GW00857437

Pete's Time-Travelling Underpants

Book 1:
RULE
BRITANNIA

Barford Fitzgerald

Pete's Time-Travelling Underpants
Book 1: Rule Britannia

My gratitude to Master Peter Tollywash for providing sketches of what he encountered on his adventures.

Note to readers

You can find more information on words in **bold** at
http://barfordfitzgerald.com/
petes-time-travelling-underpants-the-history/

Chapter 1

PETE HELD UP THE UNDERPANTS at arm's length and looked at them. They were a strange colour that wasn't quite white, but it wasn't quite yellow. They were full of holes and gave off a rather strange aroma. Pete struggled to hide the look of astonishment and disgust on his face.

"Happy birthday, Pete," Auntie Cheryl said, beaming at her godson.

"Thanks, Auntie Cheryl," Pete responded rather slowly to his godmother.

He wasn't *totally* surprised by this odd birthday present. After all, Auntie Cheryl was, as Pete's dad regularly said, 'out of her tree'. Still, even by Pete's godmother's very strange standards, this was pretty weird.

Auntie Cheryl looked at her godson, still beaming broadly. "Well, what do you think?" she asked Pete as if she expected him to throw his arms around her in gratitude.

"They're pants," Pete said. "*Dirty* pants," he added for clarity.

Auntie Cheryl's face fell. "Oh no, Pete. These are not just pants. These are Y-fronts and..." She paused and added in a whisper, "They're *magic!*" She looked at Pete, waiting to see the effect these words had on him.

She was to be disappointed.

"Oh really?" he replied sarcastically. Pete was finding it harder than usual to humour Auntie Cheryl today.

"Yeah!" Auntie Cheryl exclaimed enthusiastically, unaware of, or ignoring, Pete's sarcasm.

"Let me tell you the tale of these magical Y-fronts," Auntie Cheryl continued with a gleam in her eye and her beaming smile still on her face.

Pete rolled his eyes and put the Y-fronts down on the table next to him.

"It all started with my great-grandfather Algernon," Auntie Cheryl began in a grand voice. "He was a great explorer in Central America in the nineteenth century. A shaman sold him these ancient, magical, Mayan Y-fronts and they have been in my family ever since, passed from generation to generation." She paused and looked at Pete with wonder in her eyes.

Pete looked back at her with boredom in his.

Auntie Cheryl continued, "I have no children of my own, so as my godson you are the heir to—" She stopped and picked up the Y-fronts from the table and then almost yelled: "—these pants!"

She went down on one knee and held out the underpants to Pete.

"With these underpants comes great power and grave responsibility," she said, looking Pete straight in the eye.

"Auntie Cher, what *are* you talkin' about?" Pete asked, finally losing patience with his godmother.

She just continued in the same over-the-top voice. "As I said, the Y-fronts were bestowed upon my great-grandfather by a shaman in Belize. The secret of the Y-fronts was revealed to him by the shaman. He then passed the Y-fronts to my grandfather, who passed the Y-fronts to my father, who passed the Y-fronts to me. And now, Godson, as it is your thirteenth birthday today, your turn has come to don ... *the time-travelling Y-fronts!*"

Auntie Cheryl picked the underpants back up and put them in Pete's hands very carefully, as if they were something very valuable.

Pete stepped back and dropped them as if they were a bomb.

"You what, Auntie Cher?" Pete asked rather impolitely. "Did you say *time-travelling* pants?"

"Y-fronts, dear. And yes. But that's not all," she continued, still on one knee and picking up the pants which Pete had just dropped. "There are three things you must know about these Y-fronts, oh Pete."

She now stood up and returned to her normal voice. "Interesting Fact Number 1: They allow the wearer to time-travel," she explained. "B. They allow the wearer to understand and speak the language of wherever he may be—"

"—Ah great," Pete interrupted, "so I can wear them in French class."

Auntie Cheryl ignored the interruption and continued, "Thirdly, the Y-fronts decide where in time you will go. You may return to the present day by removing the Y-fronts. However, you cannot travel to another time period and a

7

new adventure until you complete a good deed in the period to which the Y-fronts have sent you."

She paused again and looked at Pete meaningfully and then added, "It will be your task to put right what once went wrong. To make the past a better place, one good deed at a time."

Auntie Cheryl had been telling Pete this strange tale in the dining room of Pete's house after all his birthday party guests had gone. At this point Pete's mum came in looking for her glasses (they were on her head, as usual) and Auntie Cheryl quickly put the underpants away in her pocket.

Mrs Tollywash, Pete's mother, did not see the underpants (Pete's dad always said she was blind as a bat without her glasses), which was a good thing for our story as she would almost certainly have seized the underpants and probably burned them. Mrs Tollywash was a very house-proud woman and would not have approved of dirty, hundred-year-old Y-fronts in her dining room.

Auntie Cheryl turned to Mum and said, "I must love you and leave you my daaarhh-ling." She remembered the underpants in her pocket and sneaked them back into Pete's hands while Mum wasn't looking. This time he quickly pocketed them without thinking about how disgusting they were.

Once Auntie Cheryl had left, Pete was sent to bed and that's when the real weirdness began.

Chapter 2

As Pete was getting ready for bed he found the underpants in his pocket again. He stared at the revolting article of clothing in his hand and wondered if Auntie Cheryl could have been telling the truth. He shook his head and threw the underpants into the corner of his room. How could Auntie Cheryl be telling the truth? Firstly, he knew she was insane. Secondly, whoever heard of time-travelling Y-fronts from Central America?

Pete changed into his pyjamas and was about to get into bed, when something caught his eye. It was the underpants, still lying in the corner of the bedroom where he had thrown them. They appeared to be shining in the darkness. Pete was convinced he must just be tired after the excitement of his PlayStation and Pizza party. Even so, he chuckled and said, "Let's see if the old oddball was telling the truth, then."

He picked up the underpants and held them at arm's length again. They did look pretty unhygienic. He lowered his arm and said, "*What a load of hooey,*" to himself. He was about to throw them back in the corner when he suddenly changed his mind. For some reason which he couldn't really explain, he started to put the underpants on. He gingerly stepped into them and pulled them over his pyjama bottoms (he didn't want to catch some horrible skin disease). Suddenly he felt a kind of pulling at his hips and the underpants began to glow. There was a flash of light and before he knew what was going on, he found himself outside in the dark. He was standing there in his pyjamas and, of course, the dirty old Y-fronts. A bit like Superman, but in pyjamas and dirty, old Y-fronts.

As his eyes began to adjust, he noticed he was standing by a very high wall. He turned around and saw a stone building behind him and then made out that there were bars over the windows. He then saw another building, a little further away, with a large doorway and two huge flaming torches either side.

Pete suddenly heard moaning coming from the stone building with bars over the windows and then a scream which chilled his blood. Before he had time to wonder what was going on, he heard someone shout, "Halt. Who goes there!"

He turned around to see two men with swords. One of them suddenly put his sword to Pete's neck.

"What are you doing in the residence of Noxius Maximus, Briton?" the man with the sword asked.

Pete was terrified as he stared at the man, who was wearing a helmet, old-fashioned armour and what looked to Pete like a little skirt. Pete panicked and reached down to his waist. Before the strange man could stop him, Pete had removed the time-travelling underpants. With a flash he was back in his own room, shaking all over with the underpants *and* his pyjama bottoms around his ankles (in his panic he had taken them both off).

He stood there for about five minutes, shaking and staring

into space. It's a good thing that no one walked in as Pete stood there, staring into space with no pants on.

Once he had calmed down he started walking over to his bed, but fell over flat on his face as the underpants *and* his pyjama bottoms were still around his ankles.

This time, someone did come in. Dad had been walking past Pete's room at that exact moment and had heard the bump. He opened the door and poked his head round.

"Peter, are you OK?" he asked and then saw his son, or more accurately his son's bottom. "Oh, Pete what are you doing?" he cried. "Put on your trousers, for heaven's sake!"

"What's Pete doing, Dad?" Pete could hear his brother Jim asking. Fortunately, Pete managed to pull his pyjama bottoms up before Jim also came in.

"I just fell over trying to put my pyjamas on. Leave me alone," Pete lied as his father and brother started to laugh.

"Huh, huh. Nice one, doofus!" Jim guffawed at his younger brother.

Once his loving father and brother had left the room, Pete got into bed. It took what seemed an age for him to fall asleep and when he did, he had some rather horrid dreams. He had visions of men in skirts chasing him with swords.

Pete was awoken with a start by his mother shaking him. He opened his eyes and realised he was safely in his room. *Last night must have been a dream*, he thought. He looked over towards his window and noticed the Y-fronts were still lying in the corner of his room.

It hadn't been a dream. What was even worse, it was time to get ready for school. Pete threw the Y-fronts into the bottom of his wardrobe and went to have a shower.

When Pete got home from school he decided he had to speak to Auntie Cheryl. This would mean making up a good excuse, though, so his mother didn't get suspicious (he didn't even ring his best friends usually, let alone his godmother).

"Mum! Can I ring Auntie Cheryl for some help with my History homework?" Pete bellowed down the stairs. Though Pete was lying, Mum was taken in, because Auntie Cheryl was a History teacher at another local secondary school.

"Um, yes, darling," Mum replied, shocked, but also very pleased that Pete was actually doing any homework (he didn't have any History homework, at least he didn't think he did).

When Auntie Cheryl answered, Pete told her all about the men in skirts and 'Noxius Maximus', whoever or whatever that was.

Auntie Cheryl thought for a moment and then said, "Ooh, you must have been in Roman times, you lucky boy. That's one of my favourite periods of history."

Pete wasn't quite so sure he was a lucky boy, unless Auntie Cheryl meant lucky to be alive.

"Well, you have to go back in and complete your task," she told Pete, ignoring the fact that a man had held a sword to her godson's throat.

"What? I'd rather eat broad beans than do that. I don't want to get killed by some bloke in a skirt," Pete replied incredulously.

"Don't be daft, Pete," Auntie Cheryl interjected.

Pete thought to himself that he wasn't the one being daft.

"No one can kill you when you're in the land of the underpants," she explained.

Chapter 3

"YOU WHAT?" PETE CRIED. "YOU mean like having the *Fireproof cloak of Bognagar* in *Dragon Dancer 15*?" he asked his godmother.

Now it was her turn to be confused. There was a long silence at the other end of the telephone.

Dragon Dancer, and its fourteen sequels to date, was Pete's favourite game on his Xbox (but not his favourite, favourite game—that was *Medieval Skullcrusher 8* on the Playstation). It involved taming good dragons (which you did by doing a special dance for them, hence the name) and killing bad dragons. That was about it, but it had lots of levels.

"Anyway," Auntie Cheryl went on, shaking off her godson's strange comment, "you don't need to worry. The Y-fronts make you invincible."

"Thanks, Auntie Cher. Oh, got to go, it's dinner time," Pete announced as he heard his mother calling. He abruptly put the telephone down as Auntie Cheryl tried to say good bye.

"That's *awesome!*" Pete said to himself but loudly enough for Mum to hear.

"What's awesome, dear?" she asked.

"Um, oh, um, History, Mum. Just History, it's awesome," Pete lied unconvincingly.

"OK. Glad you're enjoying it," Mum replied, nodding enthusiastically and smiling. Fortunately for Pete, she stopped there and asked no further questions. Seeing her son interested in his schoolwork was such a nice change that she didn't want to question it any further.

Pete then proceeded to wolf down his dinner, for two very important reasons:

It was pizza and Pete loved pizza.

If Pete ate it quicker, time would move quicker so it would be bedtime sooner (that's a proven scientific fact, Pete was sure of it).

Pete was keen for bedtime as this was the only time he could put on the underpants without the risk of being caught.

Sadly, Pete's theory of time speeding up if you do things quicker didn't seem to work. Instead, he just had to sit at the table longer with nothing to do while Mum and Dad droned on and on to Jim about how great the latest piece of coursework for his GCSE exams was.

Finally, bedtime did come around and Dad almost fell off his chair when Pete agreed to go without argument. Our young hero went upstairs and opened the wardrobe to find the underpants just where he had left them. He eagerly put them on over his school trousers and, before you could say 'time-travelling undergarments', the underpants began to glow and whisked Pete back to the two scary Romans, and their rather sharp swords.

He suddenly regretted his eagerness to come back to

the 'land of the underpants' as his aunt had called it. He swallowed hard and started to shake.

"Oi, Scythicus," one of the Roman guards said to the other. "'ave 'is clothes changed?"

"Don't be daft," replied the one addressed as Scythicus. "How could he have done that?"

While the two Romans argued over whether or not Pete's clothes had changed (which, of course, they had as he had been in his pyjamas before, but now was in his school uniform), Pete remembered what Auntie Cheryl had said: "The Y-fronts make you invincible."

Suddenly feeling a lot braver he said to the rather big and rather scary Roman soldier called Scythicus, "What are you going to do to me, you big girl's blouse?"

Understandably this Scythicus fellow didn't like this one bit. He raised his sword and clonked Pete on the head with the handle. Pete now found out that, although he couldn't be killed while wearing the underpants, he could still experience quite considerable pain. The underpants weren't as effective as the *Fireproof cloak of Bognagar* after all. Our hero started crying and rolling around on the floor holding his head.

"Ow! That really hurt. What did you do that for?" Pete snivelled through his tears.

The other Roman solider (the one that hadn't hit Pete over the head with his sword) guffawed just like Pete's brother Jim. "He's just a weak, little boy," he declared.

He then laughed at Pete as our hero started whimpering and whining, "I want my mummy."

Scythicus interrupted his companion's laughter. "He may

just be a weak little boy," he began slowly, "but he speaks surprisingly good Latin for a **Brittunculus**."

The underpants must be translating what I'm saying into Latin, Pete thought. In spite of this, he didn't quite understand the rather rude term that Scythicus had used for him: Brittunculus.

"This is all very suspicious," Scythicus continued. "What's he doin' hangin' around here? Let's stick him in the prison. We can decide what to do with the little rat in the morning."

The two soldiers grabbed Pete and carried him to a place which he could smell before he saw it in the moonlight. He realised it was the same stone building with the bars over the windows where he had heard the scream when he had first arrived.

"Please don't put me in there. I'm sorry for calling you a big girl's blouse earlier," he pleaded as the soldiers pulled open a rusty gate and pushed Pete into a black hole.

The underpants

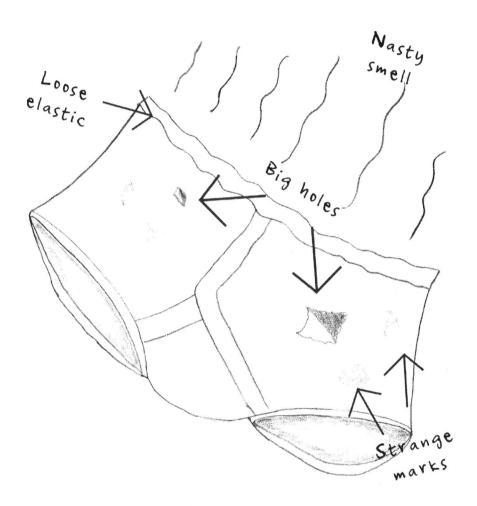

Loose elastic

Nasty smell

Big holes

Strange marks

Chapter 4

PETE FELL AND LANDED ON his bottom in something wet and cold. He really didn't want to know what it was. He couldn't see anything as there was no light in the prison. He looked round for a light switch, but then remembered that the Romans didn't have electricity.

He was about to take the underpants off again, as this was all getting a bit much, when he heard a voice from the darkness.

"Are you a Briton?" the voice asked. It sounded very strained and very old.

Pete was rather confused by this question. He thought it must just be a funny way of asking, 'Are you British?'

Pete replied to the invisible person rather nervously: "I guess so. Who are you?"

A very wrinkly and rather horrid looking face suddenly appeared next to Pete and he pulled away. This new person smelt incredibly bad and Pete was almost sick.

The man (Pete thought he was a man, but he had very, very long hair) said, "I am Quintus Nonnius of the fourth legion."

"Here we go again. Another weird name," Pete muttered to himself.

"You speak very good Latin for a Briton," the very smelly man said.

Pete was very pleased with this compliment (even though it was really the underpants that were translating his words).

"Where are we?" Pete asked.

"Do you not know, Briton? Why, you are in Noxius Maximus's prison."

Pete thought that this man spoke even more weirdly and old-sounding than his grandfather did.

"Yeah, yeah. I got that, mate," Pete told him, losing his nervousness and his patience and becoming quite cocky now. "But who is Noxius Maximus and where is his prison?"

"You are most confused, young Briton," Quintus replied, pointing out the incredibly obvious. "Noxius Maximus is the local prefect, of course, and we are in the town of **Camulodunum.**"

At first Pete thought Quintus had said, 'camel will do one', but the old man said 'Cam-oo-lo-doo-num' two more times, very slowly, as if he thought Pete was stupid. Quintus wouldn't have been wrong in most circumstances, but to be fair to Pete, in this instance he had every right to be confused.

Pete had no idea where 'Camulodunum' was. He was pretty sure it was nowhere near his hometown of Guildford, though.

Quintus then said, "I *am* surprised to meet a Briton who does not know Noxius Maximus. He is famous for his cruelty to Britons ... and for his love of *painful torture*."

"Oh brilliant." Pete sighed.

This was the last straw. Pete started to take the underpants off and, with a now familiar flash of light, found himself back in his bedroom, just as he had left it. He heaved a sigh of relief, but then noticed the wetness around his bottom again.

He took off his school trousers and realised that the smell in the prison wasn't Quintus (or at least it wasn't just him). Whatever he had fallen in when the soldiers threw him in the prison smelt worse than school dinners. He then panicked when he remembered that he would have to wear these trousers to school again tomorrow.

Chapter 5

ONCE HE HAD CALMED DOWN, Pete decided to dry the rest of his body with the dry part of his trousers. This, of course, simply served to make the trousers even wetter. He looked around his room in panic. What could he do? He couldn't give the trousers to his mother to deal with: that would arouse suspicion.

He decided to hang the trousers over the radiator. Having done this, he felt a little more relaxed and got ready for bed. He lay in bed thinking to himself. He now knew he couldn't be killed when he was time-travelling. He also now knew he could get really hurt, though, and he could really stink up his school uniform.

Next morning, Pete was awoken by the smell of his trousers. It was then he realised that putting something smelly on the radiator to dry is a bad idea! He went over to the radiator and picked up the trousers. They were stiff as a board and, by some miracle, actually smelt worse than they had last night. He then noticed his clock.

"6 am!" Pete gasped to himself.

I've never seen 6 am before, Pete thought. He couldn't believe that the smell of the trousers was that strong that it had woken him up a whole hour-and-a-half early. This did mean, though, that he had half an hour before Mum and Dad would get up.

"Brilliant! I've got time to wash them," he said to himself.

He then paused and wondered out loud, "Hang on. How do you wash something?"

Pete's mother did all his washing, so he did not have the first idea of where to start. He knew you needed water and you needed some kind of soap. He sneaked quietly into the bathroom, hoping that Mum and Dad wouldn't hear him.

He filled the basin with water, put the bar of soap in with his school trousers and sloshed them about a bit. He took the trousers out and they smelt a lot better, though still not nice. He was pretty pleased with his handiwork though. Then he realised he couldn't wear the trousers to school sopping wet.

Just as he was about to begin panicking again, he had a brilliant brainwave (at least he thought it was brilliant): Mum's hairdryer!

He found it in the bathroom cupboard and started blow-drying the trousers on the lowest setting (so he didn't wake Mum and Dad). This took rather a long time and Pete's trousers started to smell again.

He was really starting to panic when Mum walked in and found him shouting, "I hate you, you smelly scrag-buckets!" at his trousers.

"What on earth are you doing, Peter?" Mum asked as Pete turned off the hairdryer.

Pete had to think fast. "Um, I saw a small mark on my trousers so I decided to wash it off."

This didn't really explain why Pete's trousers were soaking wet and the floor was covered in water, but it was the best Pete could do.

"Oh, you silly sausage. You have made a bit of a mess," Mum replied as she took the trousers off her son. "I'm glad you are taking a bit more pride in your school uniform, but this isn't the time to wash it. I'll have to stick these in the tumble dryer for you," she concluded as she disappeared off downstairs.

It appeared that Mum had believed Pete. He was relieved that she had, but then felt slightly insulted.

"She must think I'm really thick," Pete said to himself.

But it meant that Pete had got away with it, so he did not complain.

Chapter 6

THE TROUSERS STILL SMELT PRETTY horrific when they came out of the tumble dryer. Amazingly, Mum didn't notice (possibly living with two teenage boys had caused her selectively to lose her sense of smell). Pete was so relieved that he didn't care and just put them on.

He had to run to school as he was late. When he arrived he was sweaty and out-of-breath, as well as smelly.

Even Kev, a rather smelly friend of Pete, noticed.

"Ahh, gross, Pete. Did you have an accident on the way to school or something?" Kev asked as he pinched his nose. "You smell worse than my PE bag at the end of term."

Pete was hurt by this. He had had the misfortune of smelling Kev's PE bag *during* term. He did not want to know how it smelt at the end of term.

First lesson was Computing and Pete decided to use the time to find out a bit more about Noxius Maximus. Normally he would have just played Kev at online games while Mr Briggs wasn't looking.

He opened up Wikipedia and typed in 'Noxius Maximus'. He gasped audibly as he began to read the entry.

"Woah! That guy was pretty horrible." Pete muttered out loud to himself.

Pete was right. He had probably landed in one of the worst places he could have done.

"Pete! What are you up to?" Mr Briggs asked. He had heard Pete talking to himself.

Pete quickly opened up the programming package he was meant to be looking at.

"Nothing, sir," he lied. "My computer crashed so I had to start again." Pete always told Mr Briggs this lie when he was caught playing games with Kev.

"You seem to have a lot more computer issues than the rest of the class," Mr Briggs sneered. "You are most unfortunate, Master Tollywash, aren't you?"

Once Mr Briggs had moved on, Pete reopened Wikipedia. He began to read a quote from a Roman historian called **Tacitus**:

"Noxius Maximus was well known for liking nothing better than torturing Britons," the passage began. *"Many who followed him claimed that before breakfast each day, his guards would bring five of the most wretched prisoners to the prefect."*

Pete paused and gulped. He then continued reading:

"Noxius used to enjoy taunting them about their hairstyles, putting live dormice down their tunics and even flicking the prisoners' ears until they wept most bitterly."

Pete paused and winced. He knew how this felt, as his brother Jim was also pretty keen on flicking poor Pete's ears. He continued reading again:

"Far worse, though, were the punishments his guards inflicted upon these poor Britons on Noxius's behalf."

Pete swallowed hard as he read the last bit. *The guards did even worse things to the prisoners than flicking their ears and putting live dormice down their tunics?* Pete wasn't so sure he wanted to go back now.

When Pete got home from school, it seemed the decision about whether to return to the 'land of the underpants' had been taken away from him. He went into his room and found the time-travelling underpants were missing.

Chapter 7

PETE SEARCHED ALL OVER HIS room in a panic then realised he had forgotten to put the underpants away that morning amidst the confusion of cleaning his trousers. *Mum must have found them*, he thought with a shiver. He traipsed downstairs reluctantly and went into the lounge where Mum was reading a book.

"I don't know why you seem so bothered about some manky old Y-fronts," Mum replied when Pete confronted her regarding the missing underpants.

"Anyway, where did you get them and why d'you have them?" Mum asked, peering at Pete over the top of her book.

This question stumped Pete. How could he explain in any way that wouldn't sound weird? He couldn't tell Mum the truth (she wouldn't believe him), but he couldn't think of a good reason why he had the underpants.

"They're a ... they're a ... school project," Pete stammered.

Mum looked sideways at her son and narrowed her eyes as if she were trying very hard to spot a blackhead on his nose. Her face suggested that she did not believe Pete at all, which was fair enough.

"Um, we have to grow mould on them and other things

like that so we can run an experiment at school," Pete added in desperation. Maybe if he gave more detail, then she might believe him, he reasoned.

It worked! Mum shook her head and said, "Blimey! The things you kids do at school these days, hey? There wasn't anything like that when I was a girl." She stopped talking and her face fell. "I'm afraid they're in the tip now. I went to take the garden waste just before you came home. I spotted the underpants and chucked them in with the rest of the rubbish. Sorry for ruining your project, love."

"That's OK," Pete replied smiling weakly at his mum. It had just occurred to him that this would now mean he wouldn't have to go back to Noxius Maximus's prison. Things were looking up.

"That's very mature of you, Pete," Mum commended her youngest son. "Tell you what. I'll call Miss Davidson and explain it's my fault, shall I? She can't be cross then."

Pete panicked. His Science teacher, Miss Davidson, would not have a clue what Mum was talking about and then it would all come out.

"No need to do that, Mum. I'll tell her," Pete replied with an even weaker smile.

"Oh, OK love. If you're sure." Mum gave in and went back to her book.

Pete breathed a sigh of relief. Now he wasn't going to get into trouble with Mum. Then he realised with a sigh that he had better tell Auntie Cheryl.

"I gave you a serious responsibility," Auntie Cheryl barked over the telephone when she heard about the fate of the underpants.

"They're just old pants, Auntie Cher," Pete replied, slightly less animated than his aunt.

"They may be old pants, Pete, but humanity's fate depends upon them!" she howled down the receiver.

"They're cool pants, Auntie, apart from the holes and the smell, but that's going a bit far," Pete responded. "Anyway, they can't stop me getting hurt. What's the point in that?"

"What do you mean?" Auntie Cheryl asked irritably.

"Some guy in 'pants-land'—" Pete began.

"—Land of the underpants," Auntie Cheryl corrected him.

"Yeah, whatever. Anyway, this guy hit me and it really hurt," Pete explained.

"Of course it did, Pete! The underpants make you invincible and stop you getting any serious injuries, but they can't stop you feeling *any* pain. That would be crazy," Auntie Cheryl answered, amazed by her godson's lack of understanding.

"Yeah. *Only that bit* would be crazy," Pete muttered to himself.

"What was that?" Auntie Cheryl asked sharply.

"Oh, nothing," Pete replied.

"Well, anyway. You're just lucky that I put GPS in them, aren't you?" Auntie Cheryl snapped back.

"You what?" Pete spluttered back at his aunt.

"Global Positioning System, Pete," Auntie Cheryl responded as if putting GPS in underpants was the most natural thing in the world.

"Yeah, yeah. I've heard of GPS. It's what Dad's satnav uses for directions," Pete snapped back at his auntie. He was losing patience with her craziness.

"Right, so we'll go round to the tip and find these underpants then," Auntie Cheryl confirmed.

"But they'll be long gone," Pete reasoned with his aunt. "They'll have crushed them up with everything else."

"You said your mum had only just taken them before you got home. There might still be a chance," Auntie Cheryl replied firmly.

Pete's heart sank. He wasn't too fond of the idea of returning to Noxius Maximus's prison 'for the good of mankind', or whatever Auntie Cheryl had said.

"I'll be round in the car in five minutes then," Auntie Cheryl added and then hung up before Pete could argue.

The Entrance to Noxius Maximus's hall

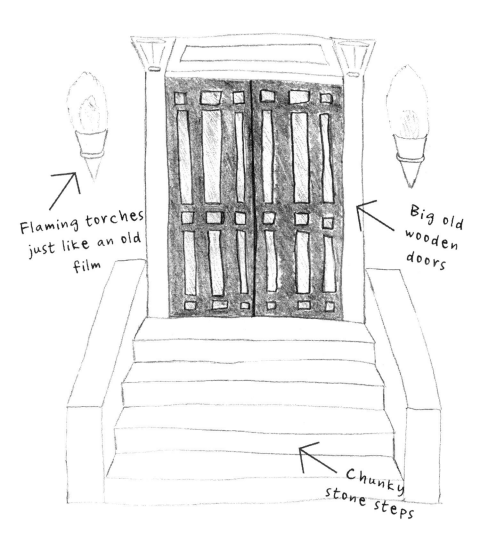

Flaming torches just like an old film

Big old wooden doors

Chunky stone steps

Chapter 8

"A UNTIE CHERYL'S GOING TO TAKE me to the tip to find the underpants, Mum," Pete said, poking his head round the kitchen door as casually as he could.

"What? I thought you were just going to tell your teacher what happened? Why's Aunt Cheryl coming?" Mum asked as she looked up from the hob with a highly confused expression.

"Uh, yeah, uh. I rang about this History homework again and then I mentioned what had happened with the pants. She reckons we can find them," Pete explained unconvincingly to his mother. "Oh, that must be Auntie Cheryl now," Pete exclaimed with clear relief in his voice as the doorbell rang.

Pete ran to the door and flung it open, but Mum made it out into the hallway before he could get outside and close it in her face.

"Oh hello, Linda," Auntie Cheryl said with surprise when her friend appeared behind Pete.

"Hi, love. Why are you taking Pete out?" Mrs Tollywash asked her oldest friend in the politest tone she could muster.

"Didn't he tell you about his school project?" Auntie Cheryl replied very naturally.

Fortunately, Pete had managed to explain to his aunt what

he had told his mother moments before Mrs Tollywash had appeared.

"Uh, yes, he did. But they're just pants!" Pete's mum replied, throwing her hands up in incredulity and abandoning her politeness.

"No, no, Linda. We cannot let young Pete down with his Science project. Anyway, we'd better go. The tip will close soon. Come on, Pete," Auntie Cheryl commanded her godson as if he were a dog, and the two of them strode off towards her car.

Mrs Tollywash stood at the door open-mouthed, watching the pair drive off.

Pete had never been to 'the tip' before. He'd heard of it, of course, but now he was going to get to know it intimately. Auntie Cheryl drove past the man on the gate, who gave them both a scowl as he looked like he was hoping to close up and go home. They pulled up next to the area reserved for non-recyclable waste and Auntie Cheryl turned off the engine.

"Great," Auntie Cheryl said clapping her hands together in satisfaction. "It seems they haven't got round to clearing it all out yet."

"So, what do we do now?" Pete asked as they both got out of the car and he saw the sea of rubbish which was so huge it seemed to disappear into the distance.

"Fear not, dear boy," Auntie Cheryl replied as she removed

her smartphone from her handbag. "Modern technology," she said cheerily as she waved her smartphone at her godson.

Auntie Cheryl moved towards Pete and showed him the screen. She tapped on an icon with the words 'Find my pants' beneath it.

"You see, my boy?" she continued with satisfaction. "It's true what they say: There's an app for that."

Pete laughed for the first time in quite a while. Then he remembered why they were there. "Right, Auntie, where are these manky pants, then?"

"That's easy, young Pete," Auntie Cheryl said as she pointed at a big blue dot on the screen that was flashing over a spot right next to where they were standing.

Pete looked over to the spot shown by the blue dot and saw the biggest pile of rubbish he had ever seen (and that included the mess in his friend Kev's bedroom).

"But, where are the pants?" Pete asked with exasperation in his voice.

Auntie Cheryl was not at all worried by this and smiled. "Oh, just somewhere in that pile of rubbish," she replied. "I've brought you some rubber gloves, my boy," she said and went into the back of her car to produce some ginormous, pink rubber gloves. "Put these on and get looking," she said.

Against his better judgement, Pete did as his godmother told him. He went over to the pile and put on the rubber gloves. He then had a strange thought: *I hope none of my mates see me.* Although, what they'd be doing hanging around the local tip at ten to five on a Tuesday, Pete had no idea.

He swallowed hard and started pulling bits out of the pile quite slowly, as he didn't want to get any of the 'rubbish juice' on his clothes (his school trousers smelt bad enough already).

Auntie Cheryl just stood at the side shouting things like, "Put your back into it," and, "Call that looking for underpants in a pile of rubbish, do you?"

It was horrible, disgusting-smelling work and after a couple of minutes Pete couldn't bear it any longer. Auntie Cheryl could see this and encouraged her godson the best way she knew how.

"Boys who don't give up get given things like the new *Dragon Dancer* game," she said with a gleam in her eye.

Pete suddenly ran into the pile and started throwing bin bags, broken toys and polystyrene packaging over his shoulder. His godmother's bribe had done the trick. Pete had to hold his breath so he didn't vomit at the smell of the rubbish.

"Oi! What do you think you're doing?"

Pete turned round to see the man from the gate a few feet away, gesticulating angrily.

Chapter 9

AUNTIE CHERYL BEGAN TO PANIC. She imagined the newspaper headlines: *Respected History teacher caught stealing from local tip.*

"To the car, Pete!" she cried, got back into the car and drove off.

She hadn't actually checked that Pete was in the car, but if she had, she would have noticed that he was most definitely not. In fact, he was standing open-mouthed next to where the car had been seconds before and had to watch as his godmother disappeared through the tip gates.

She was possibly the worst godmother ever.

The man approached and Pete thought unusually quickly for him. "I accidentally threw my phone away and the tracking app said it was here," he explained.

The man smiled and said, "Wow, modern technology, hey? I'll give you a hand." Then he paused and looked at Pete. Pete could almost hear the cogs whirring in the man's brain as something dawned on him.

"Just a sec," the man continued, "why did that lady drive off in such a hurry if that's all you're doing?"

Again, Pete thought very, very quickly by his standards

and replied casually, "She remembered she'd left a pizza in the oven."

"Oh, right." The man shrugged and turned to the pile of rubbish. "Let's find this phone then."

Pete and the man went through the pile quite quickly together. Within a few minutes Pete yelled, "Found them!" and leaped up with the pants stuck to an old loo roll and a big clump of hair.

Pete then began doing his victory dance, which he normally reserved for when he completed a level in the game *Medieval Skullcrusher 8*.

The man looked up, unimpressed by the dance and said, "That's just some disgusting old pants." He wasn't wrong, of course, and Pete remembered the lie he'd told the man about looking for a phone.

This time Pete's quick thinking abandoned him. He simply looked at the man with panic rising inside him. The man started advancing towards Pete. Pete threw the loo roll at him and shouted to himself, "Run!"

The man turned and started running away from Pete. He then realised he had no reason to run anywhere. He turned back, but by this time Pete was running out of the tip, swinging the underpants around his head.

"Come back here, you little swine!" the man shouted behind him, but Pete showed no sign of slowing down and soon disappeared out of sight.

When Pete got home he almost collapsed on the sofa. He had run nearly the whole way there, which took about twenty minutes. Normally the only running he would do would be through his avatar in the game *Goblin Quest*. Pete's avatar is a forest elf and he's six-foot-five and covered in muscles. Anyway, you don't really want to know about Pete's avatar 'Peteicus the Magnificent', so let's just get on with the tale.

"Hello, love. You're back then?" Mum asked as she came into the lounge.

It was pretty obvious he was back, as she could have heard his wheezing from a mile away.

"Uh, yeah, uh, I'm back," Pete gasped as he struggled for breath. *I really must start exercising*, he thought to himself.

"Why are you out of breath, sweetheart?" Mum asked with concern on her face.

Pete decided he couldn't tell Mum about Auntie Cheryl abandoning him. She would go ballistic on *both* of them.

"Uh, I, uh, asked, uh, Auntie, uh, Cheryl, uh, to drop me off, uh, a few blocks away," Pete spluttered. Fortunately, being out of breath had given him thinking time as he replied to his mother.

"Why's that?" Mum asked, incredibly confused.

"So I could, uh, run, uh, the last bit." Pete forced the words out of his mouth.

"Oh right, why'd you do that?" Mum asked. She'd never known her son to behave so strangely before.

"We're learning about healthy stuff at school," Pete lied. "It's good to do exercise."

Mum was so pleased that Pete was exercising that she decided not to push it any further, in case she discouraged him. "Did you find the underpants, then?" she asked.

"Yeah," Pete said, lifting the underpants up to his mother for inspection.

"Yeesh!" she exclaimed holding her nose. "Get those things away from me, Pete."

Pete limped upstairs to his room. He stood there looking at the underpants. They looked even more disgusting than before, if that was possible. He decided he wouldn't put the underpants on that night and wouldn't wash them either. That morning's excitement had taught him not to try to wash anything ever again.

He didn't put the underpants on the radiator—he'd learnt that lesson too. He hung them on his wardrobe door handle to dry off. He then sprayed them and his school trousers with a spray his mum had called 'stink-b-gon'. "I don't know why she doesn't just use that instead of washing stuff," he muttered to himself.

Chapter 10

Pete heard the telephone ring downstairs and his mum answering it. A few moments later Mum yelled up the stairs, "Pete! It's Auntie Cheryl for you!"

Pete wandered incredibly slowly downstairs to the kitchen. He didn't really want to talk to the woman who had left him to be pulverised by an angry tip worker.

"She sounds quite concerned," Mum said in a whisper so that Auntie Cheryl wouldn't hear her on the other end of the line.

"Oh, does she?" Pete asked disinterestedly.

"Yes?" Pete asked his godmother in a rather sharp tone as he took the receiver.

"Oh, thank goodness you're OK, Pete," Auntie Cheryl gushed into the phone.

No thanks to you, Pete thought.

"Yeah, just about," Pete replied impatiently.

"I'm so sorry. I thought you were in the car. I just panicked and wasn't thinking straight," Auntie Cheryl explained rather weakly.

"When *does* she think straight?" Pete wondered to himself, but did not respond to his godmother.

"You see, Pete," she continued, realising that he wasn't going to respond, "I had some 'run-ins' with the police when I was a student. I was in a protest group, you see. I was afraid that further trouble with the police might really harm my teaching career. I just panicked."

Pete didn't see at all, especially why she thought it was perfectly OK to abandon your godson. However, he thought it was easier to say that he did see.

"Fair enough, Auntie Cher." He sighed and hung up before she could go on.

Pete didn't smell as bad at school the next day. He had also slept rather well the night before, after all that running. So, Pete actually had a pretty good day at school, perhaps for the first time ever.

That evening at home passed rather uneventfully. Pete didn't hear from Auntie Cheryl again. He suspected she was leaving him alone for a bit. She had probably taken the hint from his curtness on the phone the previous day.

At bedtime, Pete went to check the underpants. They were dry and only smelt bad now, rather than 'uber-minging' as Pete would have put it. He decided it was now the right time to go back into 'the land of the underpants', as Auntie Cheryl had called it.

Pete stepped into the underpants, pulled them up to his waist and felt the familiar pull on his hips. With a flash of light, he found himself back exactly where he had been when he took the underpants off two days before. He realised that

41

time stood still in 'the land of the underpants' when he wasn't there.

Pete then heard the other prisoner, Quintus, ask him, "What are you doing?"

Although he hadn't noticed Pete disappear, Quintus had obviously heard him moving around, taking off and putting back on the underpants. Quintus was interrupted by a really horrible noise. It was like someone crying and laughing at the same time.

Then someone moaned, "Please, please! Anything but the dormice!"

Pete then heard a different voice, high-pitched and squeaky, saying, "Speak then, Briton."

Pete remembered what he had read on Wikipedia and gulped.

"What's going on, Quentin?" Pete asked his fellow prisoner.

"It's Quintus, actually," the man replied, sounding a little hurt. "Anyway, that squeaky, high-pitched voice you can hear is Noxius Maximus. The other man you can hear is a Briton like you. They think he is a *spy*."

Pete thought this sounded really cool, just like James Bond. Only this time it was with dormice.

The other man whom Noxius was torturing continued to scream, "I won't speak! I won't speak!"

Pete was now starting to get quite scared (even though at first he had thought having dormice down one's tunic just sounded itchy and annoying).

Then Noxius Maximus said, "Enough! Take him away!"

The Briton was now whimpering, "Please, no! Please, no!"

Then Pete heard a really rusty sound which he guessed was the prison door opening. The prisoner's shouts got quieter and quieter.

"What are they going to do to him, Quentin?" Pete asked with genuine concern.

"You don't want to know, Briton. It is a fate worse than dormice," Quintus replied ominously.

Pete then turned as he heard keys jingling and voices coming towards their prison cell. There was a scraping noise as the rusty bolts on the door opened and then a thin beam of moonlight shone into the cell and revealed a rat next to Pete. He screamed.

He then screamed even louder when a soldier appeared in the moonlight and yelled, "Come with us, Briton."

Pete started trying to pull the underpants off, but it was too late. Two soldiers grabbed Pete and started pushing him to the door.

Pete heard Quintus shout behind him, "I hope it's not the dormice. Or something *even worse.*"

Chapter 11

PETE BEGAN TO STRUGGLE. HE was desperate to take the underpants off now.

"Look out, Scythicus, he's trying to wriggle free!" the other guard said to his companion. They both started laughing at Pete.

They marched Pete towards the building he had seen when he first arrived: the one that was lit up with flaming torches. It was just like a film set in the 'olden days', Pete thought.

The guards pushed Pete up some stairs into a big hall. Pete saw that its walls were covered in strange paintings. What made them strange was that they were not in frames, like the ones Pete's gran had all over her lounge, but they had been painted straight on to the walls themselves. It was a bit like graffiti, Pete thought, but much prettier.

Pete noticed a man in what looked like a big dressing gown (but was actually a toga) sitting on a really big chair at the end of the room. Scythicus and his unnamed companion threw Pete on the floor in front of the man on the chair.

"**Prefect** Noxius Maximus, we bring you the new prisoner," Scythicus said to the man on the chair.

Pete looked up to see possibly the pointiest nose and

thinnest face he had ever seen. This man did not look nice. Noxius Maximus peered down at Pete. He looked like he had a bad smell under his nose (that might just have been Pete's underpants) and Pete began shaking.

"He's just a weak and rather smelly little boy," Noxius said in that horrible squeaky voice that Pete had heard earlier that morning. "Why are you wasting my time, guards?"

"We found him hiding by the outer wall of the residence. We thought he was a spy," replied the other guard, whose name Pete didn't know.

Noxius considered Pete again.

"I suppose this little runt could be a spy," Noxius sneered. "He is the last person you'd expect, after all. And he is wearing very strange clothes."

Pete was still wearing his school uniform, which looked rather out of place amongst these men in skirts and dressing gowns.

"It could be a clever trick by the Brittunculi," Noxius continued, using the same rather rude term that Pete had heard Scythicus use earlier. "But not *that* clever. They're far too stupid to get the better of *Noxius Maximus*." Noxius said his own name very emphatically and struck what he thought was a very heroic pose.

The two guards laughed and the nameless one nodded enthusiastically and said, "Yeah. They are pretty stupid aren't they, boss?"

Noxius obviously did not like this interruption.

"If I want your opinion I will ask for it, imbecile," he spat at the guard and held his hand up towards him to order silence.

"Now, you snivelling piece of dirt," he exclaimed as he turned back to Pete. "What is your name?"

"Pete," our hero responded nervously.

"How impudent. You must address me as 'Your magnificence' you little worm. Guard, strike him!" Noxius almost screamed as he leaped up from his chair.

Scythicus hit Pete round the head, but not with his sword handle this time, thankfully.

"Now, tell me again. What is your name?" Noxius squeaked at Pete.

"Um, Pete, um, your magnificence," Pete stammered.

"Umpeteum? These Britons have such *disgusting* names," Noxius sneered.

"And where are you from, *Umpeteum*?" Noxius asked with disdain.

"Guildford, your magnificence," Pete replied, rubbing his ear, which was still burning from the clip that Scythicus had given it.

"Guild-ford? Where is this *Guild-ford*?" Noxius asked, but more to the empty room than anyone in particular.

"Probably some pathetic little British settlement," the nameless guard chuckled, nodding like a dog.

"Yes, undoubtedly," Noxius replied, but he wasn't really listening to the nameless guard.

"And who is your father, *Umpeteum*? No doubt he sent you here," Noxius asked disinterestedly. He was clearly growing bored with Pete now.

"His name's Harry, your magnificence. He sells computers," Pete explained.

Noxius suddenly turned to look at Pete with a confused face. He then turned back to the guards.

"Did you hear that?" Noxius asked them. "Well he's obviously mad or stupid. I've never heard of this place 'Guildford' he talks about and he claims his father sells *artificial brains.*"

Pete realised that the word 'computers' must have been translated into Latin as 'artificial brains'. Of course! The Romans didn't have computers. *Poor things*, Pete thought.

"Release him, guards. He's no threat to us." Noxius continued waving his hand dismissively towards Pete.

Pete started crying when he heard this. These were genuine tears of joy. Pete did not know until this point that people really did cry because they were happy.

Seeing this, Noxius exclaimed, "By Jupiter, he's pathetic. Get him out of my sight."

The guards grabbed Pete again and started pushing him back out of the building.

"Where are you taking me?" Pete whined at the guards.

"Back to prison of course, you numbskull," Scythicus replied.

"Why are you taking me back to prison? He told you to let me go," Pete whimpered back to the guard.

Scythicus laughed and said to the nameless guard, "This one really is stupid." He then said to Pete, "We're just putting you back in the prison for a little while. Then we'll free you all right," he said, winking to the other guard, who laughed like a baddie in an old TV show.

Pete didn't like the sound of this one little bit.

Chapter 12

THE GUARDS THREW PETE BACK into his stinking prison cell.

He heard Quintus ask, 'What happened?', but Pete just ignored him and took the underpants off as fast as he could.

Back in his bedroom, he sat on the bed and stared into space for probably about ten minutes with the underpants around his ankles. Jim opened the door.

"What's your light still doing on? I'm telling Mum," Jim began and then stopped suddenly. He looked at Pete even more weirdly than usual. "What you got round your ankles? Ooh, is that those disgusting Y-fronts you got out the tip? Mum! Pete's sitting in his dirty Y-fronts!"

Mum came in at this point and looked at Pete sitting on the bed.

"Peter! What on earth are you wearing those things for? Take them off immediately. I will allow them in the house as they are a school project, but you must not wear them!" She then turned to Jim and said, "Thanks for telling me, son. But in future, don't tell tales on your brother."

Jim replied petulantly, "Thanks for the mixed messages,

Mum. Last time I try to be helpful!" and stormed out of Pete's room.

It was two more evenings before Pete regained the courage to return to 'the land of the underpants'. He had been eyeing the underpants warily in the intervening period, but had not felt up to facing Noxius Maximus's prison again.

When he did finally return, he found himself back with Quintus, his fellow prisoner, just as before.

"Well, what happened?" Quintus asked impatiently.

"Noxius Maximus says he'll release me," Pete replied half-heartedly.

"I wouldn't be so sure, Briton," Quintus warned him. "I was told I would only be in here for six months, but here we are two years later."

"Oh, right." Pete sighed. *Coming back maybe wasn't a great idea*, he thought. "What are you doing in here, Quentin?" he asked after a pause.

"I was once an officer in the Roman Army and was highly respected. But then Noxius Maximus became prefect and things changed." Quintus sighed.

"Oh, OK," Pete replied, thinking Quintus had stopped talking.

"Yes, Noxius is a cruel man. I refused to torture the local people as he ordered and I was put in prison for it," Quintus continued.

Pete was very confused by this. If someone had said to him, "Look, mate. You can either put dormice down this

49

person's jumper or I'll put you in a prison which smells of pee," he knew he'd have chosen the dormice. But clearly Pete and Quintus were two very different people.

It was still dark outside and Pete managed to fall asleep in spite of the smell and the rats. He was awoken in daylight by a guard kicking him.

"It's time, you worthless Brittunculus," the guard shouted at Pete. He picked Pete up and shoved him towards the prison cell door.

"Fare thee well, young Briton. I hope they do free you," Quintus said to Pete.

The guard pushed Pete along in front of him towards some big gates made of big pieces of wood. They looked a bit like his granddad's shed door, Pete thought, just a lot bigger. The guard asked another guard to let him and Pete through. This other guard removed an enormous chain and the gates were pushed open.

Pete's heart sank as he was led over to a horse cart where a man was standing with a whip. Pete started to struggle.

"What are you doing? Let me go!" Pete squealed as he tried to get free from the guard's grip.

The man with the whip came towards them and said, "It's hardly worth me coming out here for this," and looked Pete up and down. "He is dressed rather funny, isn't he?"

"What's he talking about?" Pete whimpered at the guard.

The guard ignored him and just said, "Silence, slave."

Chapter 13

PETE SUDDENLY FELT BRAVE, FOR some stupid reason, and said, "What do you mean 'slave'? I thought you were setting me free? Anyway, I'm not the one who's dressed funny."

The two men said nothing. The guard just clipped Pete round the ear and pushed him down in front of the man with the whip.

"Get into the cart, slave," the man with the whip said.

The guard grabbed Pete again and threw him down next to the cart.

"Get in," the guard said and, feeling less brave this time, Pete decided to listen and climbed in to the back of the cart.

"Where are you taking me?" Pete asked the man with the whip.

"Where all slaves go, of course. To the slave market," the man barked as if it were the most obvious thing in the world. The cart then pulled away.

Sitting on the floor of the cart was even less comfortable than being driven in Pete's big sister Susie's thirty-year-old Ford Fiesta over speed bumps.

The cart drove through streets that smelt almost as bad as the prison. The streets were made of large pieces of stone with gutters down the middle. There was some really nasty stuff flowing in those gutters. There were a few stone buildings either side of the road.

Pete saw a man being carried out of one of the buildings by four other men. He appeared to be sitting on a chair that was carried on a stretcher and the four men were supporting the stretcher on their shoulders. The man on top of the thing like a stretcher (which was actually called a '**sedan chair**', but Pete did not know this) was wearing a toga just like the one Noxius Maximus wore. The men carrying the sedan chair were wearing what looked like very shabby and long T-shirts with a belt around the middle and rather baggy and itchy-looking trousers. The cart stopped to allow the man in the sedan chair to go in front.

"Good morning, sir," the man driving the cart said.

The man in the sedan chair looked vaguely in his direction and then turned away. Another cart passed Pete on the other side of the road. It was full of barrels. Soon Pete noticed that the buildings looked less grand and were now made out of wood with thatched roofs. They were a little like his grandparents' cottage in the countryside, but nowhere near as nice.

They finally stopped at a place where people were standing around shouting a lot. In the middle of them were lots of people in chains and near them a wooden stage. It looked a little bit like the summer fair at school, Pete thought, especially with all the miserable faces. He realised this must be the slave market and the people in chains must be the slaves.

The man with the whip opened up the cart and told him

to get down. Pete got down pretty slowly, as his hands were tied together and it was difficult to balance. The man then tied his wrists to the back of the cart. Pete was beginning to think that Auntie Cheryl had given him the worst birthday present ever.

The man with the whip went over to a very, very fat man who was wearing what looked like a bed sheet, but was actually a gigantic toga, wrapped round him. They started talking to each other quietly and then they looked over at Pete and both laughed.

The very, very fat man in the bed sheet then said loudly, "Bring the boy over to the other slaves."

For a split second Pete thought he might be freed as the man untied him. But then he pulled out some handcuffs which were attached to a chain and led Pete over to the other slaves, who were all chained up to a post. He chained Pete to the post as well.

Although Pete really wanted to, because his hands were chained he couldn't take the underpants off and go home. After a short while Pete began to be quite interested in what was going on around him.

He looked round at the other slaves and saw men, women and children, many even younger than him. They were all sitting on the ground looking down at their feet and some of the children were crying.

It was simply horrible. That was all that could be said.

A man walked up to the crowd of slaves and began placing something around each of their necks. As the man came closer, Pete could see that they were some sort of sign attached to string. The man approached Pete and placed a sign over his head.

"Oi! What's all this-" Pete began to protest, but the man had already moved on to the next slave. Pete looked down at the sign. It was made of what looked like very thick paper made of wood shavings. He read the sign:

"Briton. Male. 12-14 years-old. Good for unskilled tasks requiring little thought."

Unskilled tasks? Requiring little thought? The cheek! Pete thought to himself.

Men in togas then started to walk up and look at these unfortunate chained-up people. Pete could hear them making comments to each other as if the slaves couldn't hear them. This was almost right, as Pete was the only one there who could properly understand the Latin these men were speaking. The rest of the slaves were local Britons who spoke little or no Latin.

"This ugly one looks rather strong," one man said to another, pointing to a large muscular man next to Pete. "I expect he could keep the rest of my slaves in line."

The other man agreed. "Yes. I need another slave to carry me to town. One of mine just died, rather annoyingly. This one might do the job."

Pete couldn't believe the way these two men were talking about these other human beings who were chained up before them. He could feel anger rising inside him. He then almost boiled with rage when he then saw one of the men in togas put his hands to the muscular slave's face and open his lips up. He then peered into his mouth and said, "Hmmm. Pretty good teeth this one's got." The muscular man whose mouth was being inspected obediently stood there while this took place.

Once the men in togas had moved on, the big, muscular man turned to Pete and asked, "Where are you from? Your clothes are very strange."

Pete suddenly snapped out of his angry trance, slightly startled at being spoken to. He answered the muscular man who, just like Noxius Maximus, replied that he had never heard of Guildford.

"And what's your name, stranger?" the big, muscular man continued.

"Pete," our hero answered.

"That's an odd name. You're not an Iceni, then?"

Pete didn't know what this word 'Iceni' (which Pete had heard as Eye-keeni) meant, but he was pretty sure he wasn't one.

"Well, Pete. My name is Brennus," the man explained.

Pete thought Brennus probably won the odd name competition, not Pete.

"I was once a famous warrior. The Romans feared me. Now I am just a slave." Brennus sighed and looked down at his feet.

The man with the whip came over and said, "Get up, you miserable bags of bones." He pulled Brennus up by the chain. Then all the slaves stood up and some other men came and helped the man with the whip unchain them. The slaves, including Pete, were led over to the stage. They were then chained up again next to it.

Brennus and three other slaves were chained up on the stage. A crowd of men in tunics and togas (or dresses and bed sheets as they appeared to Pete) gathered at the front of the stage and started looking at the slaves and talking to each other.

Pete did not like the look of this one bit.

Chapter 14

THE VERY, VERY FAT MAN in the very, very large toga came onto the stage and cried, "The market is now open. Our first slave is a Briton, twenty-five years of age, ideal farm worker, very strong. I will start the bidding at 2,000 sesterces."

There was a lot of grumbling from the men and then someone finally put a bid in. Eventually the bidding finished and the first slave was sold. He was then taken away to the side of the stage to the man who had bought him.

Pete thought that this was just like those auction programmes that his grandma liked, where people try to sell the old rubbish from their loft. But sadly it was people being sold, not rubbish from the loft.

He suddenly felt the anger increasing inside him again and began to feel very brave. Then he had a thought: maybe his task was to help free these poor people. He remembered a song he'd sometimes heard called 'Rule Britannia'. He didn't know why, but he thought singing it might help. So, he started singing and banging the side of the stage:

"Rule, Britannia.
Britannia rules the waves.

Britons never, never, never,
Shall be slaves."

The very, very fat man stopped as he was about to introduce the next slave and looked at Pete with his mouth open. So did all the men who had been bidding except one man who was laughing very loudly and looking at Pete. The rest of the slaves also looked at each other open-mouthed.

Then Brennus stood up and started singing with Pete and soon all the slaves were on their feet singing.

The very, very fat man shouted, "Deal with them!" to a group of men at the side of the stage. They came over and hit Pete and Brennus over the head. Pete fell down and started crying and everyone else stopped singing.

One of the men said to Pete, "You'll regret that, slave," and unchained him. He then dragged him back over to the cart and he was locked up inside again.

Pete realised that that probably wasn't the cleverest or most helpful thing he could have done. In any case, if he'd hoped to free the slaves and complete his task, he had failed miserably.

A woman and a little girl were dragged onto the stage next. The little girl, who Pete thought was probably only about seven, was in floods of tears. The very, very fat man continued: "A mother and daughter being sold as a pair. Excellent kitchen staff. Though she is just a Briton, the mother is skilled in making dishes just like in Italy."

Bidding began and the little girl wept even more bitterly. Pete could feel his anger returning, but he knew that there was nothing he could do for now. Finally, the bidding ended and the mother and daughter were led away to their new owner, who was handing money to a man by the side of the stage.

Pete then saw Brennus being dragged to the centre of the stage as the next slave for sale. Pete could see that he wasn't lying when he said he was a warrior. He looked like one of the *Mystic Hero-Sorcerers* from Pete's *Dragon Dancer* computer game, with muscles as big as Pete's head. There were lots of men trying to buy him and he sold very quickly.

While this was going on, our young time-traveller noticed the man with the whip talking to another man nearby. They were both looking at him. Pete recognised the other man as the man who had been laughing when Pete was singing.

They both walked over to Pete and the man with the whip said, "You're very lucky, you little toad. This man has agreed to buy you. If not, you'd have probably gone back to rot in the prefect's prison."

The man with the whip then opened up the back of the cart, grabbed Pete and threw him down at the feet of the other man.

"Well you're a rather amusing little Briton, aren't you?" the other man said to Pete with a chuckle. "I'm sure I'll find a good use for you on my estate."

Chapter 15

PETE DIDN'T KNOW WHETHER TO be scared or relieved that this man had bought him. He seemed nicer than the man with the whip, but that wasn't hard.

The man told Pete to follow him and they both walked over to a very skinny, bald man with a big, hooked nose. He was wearing a very dirty tunic.

"Snottius. I've just bought this boy," the man explained. "Take him back to the estate and put him to work in the kitchens. I think cook could do with some extra help."

This Snottius character looked at Pete in a rather unfriendly way and then said, "Of course, Master. I'm sure we will find some fitting work for this runt."

"I'll be back before nightfall. I have other business to attend to here in town," Snottius's master, who Pete guessed must now be his master too, said and walked off back towards the market.

"So, what's your name, rat-face?" Snottius asked.

Pete could tell that Snottius didn't like him and he had decided that the feeling was mutual.

"Pete," our hero replied.

"What kind of a name is that?" Snottius sneered. "You

Britons have some funny names." He paused. "And some *funny* clothes," he added, inspecting Pete's school uniform with disdain. "We'll have to get rid of those."

Pete's bravery returned again. He decided he wasn't going to be bullied by this skinny weed. "Well what are you, then? Snottius is a pretty stupid name!" Pete stated boldly.

Snottius was not impressed at all by this.

"I am a Gaul, you little hamster-bum, and worth a hundred times what I imagine Master just paid for you. In fact, I wouldn't be surprised if the slave-dealer paid him to take you away." Snottius leaned in with his face right next to Pete's as he said this. Pete caught a whiff of breath which probably didn't smell all that different from hamster-bum.

Pete thought to himself that he'd heard of the Gauls from his *Asterix* comic books. They'd all seemed pretty cool in those. Shame Snottius wasn't like them.

"Anyway," Snottius continued, "I am a very busy man, so let's just get you back to the estate."

Snottius then led Pete to another cart and ordered him to climb onto the back of it. This was pretty hard to do, as Pete was still wearing the handcuffs. Snottius then tied Pete to the side of the cart and got onto the front.

He drove the cart along more roads made of stones and past more wooden, thatched buildings. The buildings ended quite quickly and soon they were out in the countryside. They were driving for what seemed like ages and there was nothing around except trees, bushes and sometimes a field. It was really boring. In fact, it made Guildford look like Las Vegas.

The stone road ended and they travelled on a very rocky

dirt-track. Pete was thrown around in the back of the cart. They passed some men in dirty tunics working in a field and then Pete saw some small wooden buildings. Finally, Snottius stopped the cart outside a stone building.

"Right, we're here," Snottius announced. He then came round to the back of the cart and untied Pete. "I will take you to cook and he can decide what to do with you," Snottius said. After a pause he continued, "If he's got any sense, he'll probably just chop you up with the rest of the offal."

Pete didn't know what offal was, but he didn't like the sound of being chopped up with it.

"But, I thought Master told you to find me a job," Pete whined back to Snottius.

"He did. And I said I'd find you something fitting. Being fed to the master's dogs is probably the most fitting job I can find for you." Snottius saw that Pete was scared and started laughing. He breathed in a fly and then started coughing and couldn't stop. Pete thought that served him right.

Snottius took Pete into the kitchen. It was dark and only a small amount of light was coming from the tiny windows and from a fire with a pot over it. As Pete's eyes became accustomed to the light he saw a man in the shadows. The man had a huge beard, a huger belly and an even huger knife. As he emerged from the shadows, Pete saw that there was blood all down his front. Pete screamed and the man with the huge belly started laughing. He then saw Snottius and the laughter stopped immediately.

"What do you want and who is this boy?" the man with the huge belly snapped at Snottius. Pete could tell from the way he spoke to Snottius that this man with the big belly didn't like him either.

"Fresh meat from the slave market. Master bought him today and wants you to find some use for him," Snottius told him.

"Oh, I'll definitely find a use for him." The cook laughed and waved his knife at Pete.

Snottius

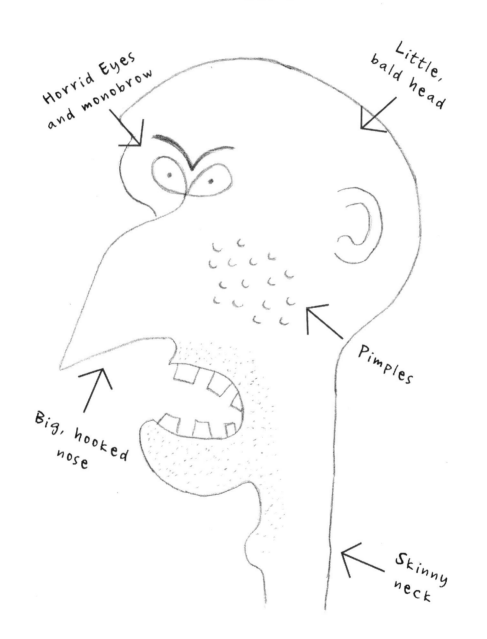

Horrid Eyes and monobrow

Little, bald head

Pimples

Big, hooked nose

Skinny neck

Chapter 16

S NOTTIUS SNORTED AND SAID, "WHATEVER. Just don't bother me with him. Oh, and get him some proper clothes."

With that, Snottius left the kitchen and the man with the big belly turned to Pete. Pete swallowed very hard and took a step back.

"I'm invincible, I'm invincible," Pete kept muttering to himself under his breath, but it gave him no more courage.

"Do not be afraid, youngster," the man with the big belly said with a chuckle, "unless you're a tasty chicken."

The joke didn't make Pete any less scared. He didn't say anything. He just kept his eyes fixed on the huge knife in the man's hand.

"So, what is your name, boy?" the man asked.

Pete decide to break his silence as he definitely wanted to keep on the right side of this scary-looking man who was holding a knife.

"Pete, sir," Pete squeaked. He could hardly get the words out.

"An odd name, boy. Never heard one like it before. Anyway, my name is Caradocus," he said putting the knife out towards Pete.

Pete shrieked, "Please don't kill me!"

Caradocus looked confused and then looked down at his hand. He realised he was still holding the knife. "Oops, sorry Pete," he apologised as he wiped the blood off his knife onto his apron and put the knife down. He then put his hand out again to shake hands with Pete.

Pete felt a little more confident now that Caradocus had put the knife down. He shook hands with the cook and said, "P-p-pleased to meet you, sir."

Caradocus laughed again. It was a very deep, good-natured laugh which made his huge belly shake.

"Welcome, Pete. You are now part of the household of Probus: he is our master," Caradocus explained while sitting down on a stool and beckoning to Pete to do the same. "Probus is a merchant and landowner from Rome," he continued. "Life is generally good here. We are some of the luckier slaves, if I'm honest. Probus is generally a fair master."

Pete sat in silence listening to Caradocus. He was exhausted from the events of the day so far and could not really take much in.

"Oh, just watch out for that Snottius," Caradocus warned Pete. "The man is a prize weasel-head and thinks he's much better than us Britons."

Pete nodded along as Caradocus spoke, but still said nothing.

"Anyway, can't sit around all day nattering." Caradocus sighed. "We'd better get you out of those things," he said, pointing at the handcuffs which Pete had forgotten he was still wearing. "Then we can get you to work," Caradocus concluded with a nod.

The cook disappeared out of the kitchen and Pete heard him talking to Snottius, whose whiny voice Pete could recognise. The conversation did not sound friendly, but eventually Caradocus reappeared with a key and removed Pete's handcuffs.

"Thanks, Caradocus," Pete said as he stood up and rubbed his wrists where the handcuffs had been.

Pete looked around the kitchen and swallowed hard. He saw dead animals hanging upside down and then he almost screamed when he saw what was on the table behind where Caradocus had been standing. It looked like it had been a rabbit before, but it was looking pretty gross now. Caradocus noticed that Pete was staring at the rabbit on the table and mistook his disgust for hunger.

"Sorry Pete, that's not for your dinner I'm afraid." Caradocus laughed, setting his belly off shaking again.

Pete was pretty relieved to be honest: he much preferred pizza and fish fingers.

"Right," Caradocus said emphatically, clapping his hands together, "I'll just get Julius and we can get you to work."

Chapter 17

CARADOCUS DISAPPEARED AGAIN AND PETE thought that now was the time to take off the underpants. He stopped just as he was about to do so. He was intrigued to see who Julius was. Caradocus reappeared with a boy who looked about Pete's age. He was blond and a little taller than Pete.

Caradocus said, "Julius, this is Pete. I'd like him to work with you."

Julius just replied, "Of course, Caradocus." And nothing else.

After a pause, Caradocus asked, "Have you eaten, Pete?"

Well, of course, Pete hadn't. Not in prison and definitely not at the slave market.

"I'll get you something," Caradocus said and went over to the big fireplace with a large metal pot hanging in the middle of it. He started stirring the pot. Pete thought he would try to 'break the ice' with Julius.

"Where are you from, Julius?" he asked the new boy.

Julius wasn't keen to speak it seemed. He simply replied, "Here."

The two boys sat there in silence while Caradocus stirred the pot. Then the cook came over with a bowl and put it down in front of Pete. The bowl contained hot, grey water with bits in it. It made school dinners look like a *Meat Feast* pizza from Gino's Pizza Company (Pete's favourite).

Remembering that he was invincible in 'the land of the underpants', he decided to give this dubious-looking, grey soup a taste. It didn't taste very bad, but it didn't taste very good either. Even though he was hungry, Pete could only eat about half of it before he just got bored.

Julius said, "Right. Are you finished? Let's go then." He didn't sound like he really wanted to work with Pete.

Pete followed Julius out of the kitchen and Caradocus shouted after them, "Julius! Can you find Pete a tunic, please? And good luck, young Pete!"

"Strange clothes you've got on," Julius commented over his shoulder as he led Pete into what looked like a storeroom and started looking around for something. "Got it!" Julius said emphatically as he pulled a piece of material out of a box and handed it to Pete. "Put that on, then," he ordered Pete impatiently and left the room.

Pete held up the piece of material—it looked like a huge T-shirt, but it was made out of very itchy material. "This must be a tunic, then," Pete muttered to himself. Pete put it down and removed his school shirt.

He then pulled down the time-travelling underpants and found himself in his bedroom. He paused for a second, feeling slightly surprised and then said, "Oh, yeah!" as he realised why he was back in his room. He undressed quickly and then put the time-travelling underpants back on over his own underpants.

He was whisked back to the small room where Julius had

left him and saw the tunic. He put it on over his head and stood in the room, wondering what to do next. Before long, though, Julius returned.

"You're done, then?" he asked, but before Pete could reply, he said, "You'll need this," and handed Pete a piece of cord.

Pete looked at him blankly and then stared at the piece of cord.

"Well, tie it round your waist, you prune," Julius prompted Pete impatiently.

Pete did as he was told then Julius said, "Follow me. We'd better go to the granary," and led him into a room that was open to the outside, as two huge doors on the far side had been flung open. A rather cold wind was blowing in and Pete shivered. Julius looked at him with undisguised disgust.

"Right, you'd better help me with the wheat, then," Julius said to Pete while leading him over to a big, circular box in the middle of the room. Pete peered in and saw that it was filled with lots of little brown things. He guessed this must be wheat, as he didn't think he'd ever seen any before.

"We've got to separate all this wheat from the chaff," Julius explained to Pete. Pete didn't know what chaff was or how you separated it from wheat. Julius guessed this when he looked at Pete's face.

Julius rolled his eyes and said, "You don't know how to do that, do you?" He sounded like Pete's brother Jim when he asked him for help with homework. Jim was so patronising that Pete hardly ever asked for help. In fact, Pete believed it was his brother's fault (rather than because of his own laziness) that he rarely did his homework at all.

Julius took out what looked like a big tambourine and

scooped up the brown stuff. He walked outside where the wall was missing and then threw the brown stuff up in the air. Some bits of it blew away and other bits fell at his feet. He handed Pete the tambourine thing and said, "You try."

Pete scooped up some of the brown stuff and started walking towards the outside area. He was concentrating so hard on carrying the big tambourine thing and not dropping any wheat that he didn't notice the step down.

"Watch out for the step, you pill—"

But Julius's warning came too late and Pete ended up with the tambourine on his head and the wheat all around him on the floor. At this point the wind picked up again and blew most of the wheat away.

Pete lifted up the tambourine thing and looked at Julius, who was just staring at him and not saying a word. Pete thought that maybe this was a good time to go back home for the time being. He removed the underpants and before he knew it, he was back in his bedroom.

Chapter 18

H E REMOVED HIS TUNIC QUICKLY and took his pyjamas from under his pillow. He dressed and then paused, looking at the tunic on the floor: he would need to find somewhere to hide it. Finally, he opted for under his mattress. He folded the tunic up, placed it under his mattress and then slumped down on his bed.

He quickly fell into a deep sleep after the excitement of his latest trip to the 'land of the underpants'. His bed had never felt so comfortable.

The next evening, after school, he called Auntie Cheryl and told her all about the prison, the slave market and Snottius, Caradocus and Julius.

"Wow, Pete," Auntie Cheryl replied enthusiastically. "That sounds fantastic. I'm so jealous, but I suppose I must let the next generation have their turn."

Pete didn't think Auntie Cheryl was being that selfless. He'd happily have let her swap with him in the prison!

"Yeah, it is kind of fun, but I'm getting a bit bored. I

don't know what the good deed I need to complete is," Pete complained to his godmother.

"Ah, well, Pete, your task may not become apparent for some time and it may take even longer to complete it," she explained.

Pete was far from impressed: his godmother hadn't explained that bit at the start.

"Just think of it like a mission in that fairy dancing game you like," Auntie Cheryl reasoned with her godson.

"*Dragon Dancer*, you mean," Pete quickly corrected her. Fairy dancing? How dare she suggest such a thing.

"Whatever," Auntie Cheryl continued, "but it's basically like that."

"I suppose you're right, Auntie Cher," Pete begrudgingly agreed.

"And think of the hours you waste, I mean spend, playing that game," she continued. "Also, you'll just return to the same time and place here as when you went into 'the land of the underpants', so you aren't missing out on anything here."

"Yeah, I guess, but I can't get hurt playing *Dragon Dancer* or be covered in gross-smelling stuff," Pete argued with some justification.

"Anyway, just stick with it, Pete, and keep me posted. Let me know if you have any questions, love. I better go, anyway. It's parents' evening at school. Bye." And with that Auntie Cheryl hung up. Pete often forgot that Auntie Cheryl was a supposedly mature and respectable teacher.

As Auntie Cheryl predicted, the next couple of trips back to the first century AD dragged on and were quite boring really—not exactly like *Dragon Dancer*. Pete managed to master separating the wheat from the chaff in the end, although he probably had to spend four hours doing it before he got anywhere.

He also had to help in the fields collecting more wheat in—that was horrendous. Pete hadn't realised work could be so hard.

"You can't expect me to do this!" Pete exclaimed after about five minutes of gathering in wheat.

"Oh, I'm sorry, young sir," Snottius sneered sarcastically. "Of course, you do have a choice," the chief slave continued, smiling crookedly. "You can either do it or I'll beat your bottom black and blue," he barked at Pete.

Pete swallowed hard and decided it was better just to get on with it.

Julius smirked at Pete's very public dressing-down. Even so, the young Briton decided to give Pete an extra hand. He even started talking to Pete and after a few days of working together on the farm they were becoming quite good friends.

"What do you do for fun round here?" Pete asked Julius one day.

"Fun? There isn't much," Julius replied. "Only thing is playing pranks on 'snot-for-brains', but I almost never get to do that."

"Snot-for-brains?" Pete repeated enquiringly to his friend.

"Oh, that's what I call Probus' son, Superbus, although not to his face of course," Julius explained.

One other thing that made the next few days a little more interesting was the discovery of a rather tasty snack: **dormouse dipped in honey**. Caradocus let Pete have one that was left over after one of Master Probus's dinners.

"They're a real delicacy," Caradocus assured Pete as he passed him the roasted rodent.

Pete scrutinised the 'delicacy'. It looked rather like a very small roast chicken. He decided to give it a go to avoid hurting Caradocus's feelings. His face brightened as he bit into it.

"Good, eh?" Caradocus asked with a grin.

Pete nodded enthusiastically. These tasty rodents now became an obsession for our young time-traveller.

Probus's house

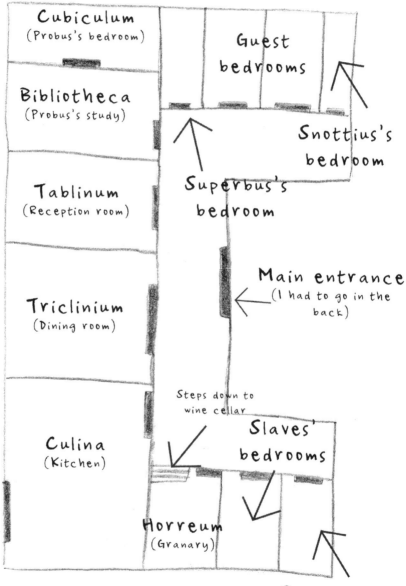

Cubiculum (Probus's bedroom)

Guest bedrooms

Bibliotheca (Probus's study)

Snottius's bedroom

Tablinum (Reception room)

Superbus's bedroom

Triclinium (Dining room)

Main entrance (I had to go in the back)

Steps down to wine cellar

Slaves' bedrooms

Culina (Kitchen)

Horreum (Granary)

Storeroom (Our bedroom)

Chapter 19

"**D**o you want to know a secret, Pete?" Julius asked one evening as they were both going to sleep on their straw mattresses. They both had to sleep on this rather uncomfortable bedding on the floor of a storeroom next to the kitchen.

"What?" Pete whispered back in the darkness, so as not to wake anyone.

"Julius isn't my real name," Pete's new friend explained. He then paused a second and his voice dropped so low that Pete now struggled to hear him. "It's Caratacus," Julius continued.

"Oh, OK," Pete replied as if Julius had just told him something rather boring like, "I don't like strawberries—I actually like raspberries."

After a silence Julius continued, "You know, like the famous king who fought the Romans."

Of course, Pete did not know about this famous king. He knew even less about the history of Britain than he did about washing trousers.

"Oh, cool," Pete replied, actually a little disappointed by this secret. "Why are you called Julius then?"

"Because Probus didn't want to have a slave with the name of a famous, heroic British king," Julius explained with clear pride in his real name. "But that's not the real secret, Pete," the blond-haired boy continued, dropping his voice so low now as to be almost inaudible. "Do you know who my auntie was?"

Pete genuinely did not know, but he hoped she was a better aunt than Auntie Cheryl.

"It was Boudicca!" Julius whispered with a sound of awe in his voice.

"Oh, right," Pete replied. "Who was Boo-di-kah?"

Julius giggled now. "Oh Pete, you really are a bit thick, aren't you?"

Pete was hurt by this. However, it was the fact that Julius (or should I say Caratacus?) thought that Pete was a bit stupid that had made him start to like this new addition to Probus's household in the first place. He found Pete entertaining.

"She was Queen of the Iceni, of course!" Julius continued.

There was that 'Eye-keeni' word again that Brennus had used at the slave market.

"Who are the Iceni, Julius?" Pete asked.

"You obviously aren't from around here." Julius chuckled. "*We* are the Iceni, of course, and Boudicca was our queen."

"Ah cool, so you're kind of like a prince, then?" Pete asked.

"I *am* a prince. But no one believes me." Julius sighed.

"So where is your aunt now? And your parents?" Pete asked his friend. He realised he hadn't met Julius's parents and he hadn't wondered why until now.

"Dead, I think," Julius said with sadness in his voice.

"The Romans killed Boudicca after her rebellion. I haven't seen my father since I was tiny and I never met my mother."

"Oi, you two. Shut up!"

Snottius's familiar nasal whine came from the darkness. Both boys fell silent. Pete lay in the dark thinking about what his new friend had told him. Then a thought hit him. This was his mission: to free Julius and lead an army against the Romans!

Pete lay awake for most of the night, plotting how he might do this. When he did finally fall asleep, he dreamt of himself leading an army against the Romans, who were led by Noxius Maximus. Noxius kneeled down before Pete and whimpered pitifully.

"Please spare me, your magnificence," Noxius whined.

When Pete woke up, he decided he should talk to Auntie Cheryl about this.

Chapter 20

BACK IN TWENTY-FIRST CENTURY GUILDFORD, Pete rang Auntie Cheryl. He explained what Julius had told him and what he thought his task should be.

"I dunno, Pete. I don't think you *are* meant to lead a rebellion against the Romans. I mean, they were pretty ruthless with poor Boudicca," Auntie Cheryl told him once he had finished his highly excited explanation.

"No fair!" Pete whinged back at his godmother.

"But I reckon you might be there to free Julius," Auntie Cheryl continued.

"Cool. So how might I do it, d'you reckon?" Pete asked his aunt, his enthusiasm now returned.

"Well, Pete, you could dress up as the ghost of Boudicca and scare everyone. Julius could escape while everyone's running away in fear," Auntie Cheryl suggested.

Pete groaned. "Really, Auntie Cher, that's an awful idea."

"OK. OK. I'm just thinking. Ooh, how about robbing money from the slave dealer who sold you? You could then buy Julius's freedom," she replied.

"What?" Pete asked incredulously. "How am I going to do that?"

"Well, you could put on a mask and threaten the slave dealer with a big stick," Pete's godmother suggested, a little offended at the treatment Pete was giving to her ideas.

Pete wondered to himself what planet Auntie Cheryl was on. It definitely wasn't planet earth.

"Won't everyone wonder where I got all that money from?" Pete asked, rather sensibly. "Ooh, I've got an idea. What if I gave everyone sleeping tablets and then just sneaked out? But where would I get the sleeping tablets from?"

"A-ha!" Auntie Cheryl cried. "Do they have big jars of wine in the house?"

"Uh, yeah," Pete replied, confused as to why his auntie should be interested in where they kept their wine.

"Right. They're called an *amphora*," Auntie Cheryl continued.

"Thanks for the history lesson, but how does this help?" Pete asked rudely.

"You could sneak Julius out in one of those!" Auntie Cheryl exclaimed in triumph.

"You might be on to something there, Auntie Cher. It's definitely better than the Boudicca ghost idea."

And so Pete and Auntie Cheryl settled on this as their great escape plan.

Back in the first century AD, Julius wasn't 100 per cent convinced by Pete's escape plan. Something seemed not quite right with it, but he decided to give it a try. Having told

Pete about his family history the other evening, his desire for freedom had been rekindled.

So, after Julius and Pete had helped with serving dinner to their master and his family, they sneaked into the wine cellar. They found an empty amphora. It was very heavy and they both had to strain themselves to lift it to confirm it was empty.

This was where the plan hit an unforeseen snag.

"How am I going to fit in there?" Julius asked, pointing at the thin neck of the amphora.

"Let's just take the top part of the neck off, put you in, and then put the top back on," Pete suggested with a big smile.

Julius wasn't quite so impressed with this brainwave, but agreed to help Pete find something to take the top off with.

"There's a slave who does all the woodwork for the estate called Marrecus. He has a workshop full of tools. Maybe we can cut the top off with his saw?" Julius suggested.

So they both crept out of the wine cellar to make their way to the workshop. Then Julius paused at the top of the stairs.

"Hang on. How on earth are you going to move it with me inside?" Julius asked. "The two of us found it hard enough to lift just now when it was empty."

"Oh, yeah," Pete replied, as he too stopped in the corridor just ahead of Julius. Before Pete could properly consider this new problem, he saw a familiar hooked nose coming round the corner at the end of the corridor.

"It's Snottius," he whispered to Julius and tried to push

him back into the cellar, but they both tripped and fell down the steps, straight into the amphora.

The amphora wobbled and both boys stared at it, unable to move from the heap in which they had fallen at the bottom of the stairs. Finally, the amphora fell over. It cracked down the middle, and its top part broke off, but not in the way they'd had in mind. This caused so much noise that Snottius couldn't help but hear them. He appeared at the top of the steps and looked down at the two boys with an awful grin on his face.

Chapter 21

"WHAT'S GOING ON DOWN HERE then, my little friends?" Snottius asked very slowly and in a tone that suggested maybe they *weren't* friends.

Snottius started coming down the stairs and Pete scrambled to hide behind a piece of broken amphora. It wasn't really big enough, in fact it only just about hid Pete's head.

"So, you little wastrels," Snottius spat, "shirking your duties and breaking perfectly good amphorae. You'll have to pay for that."

Julius was on his knees in front of Snottius, pretty much exactly as he had ended up when he fell down the stairs. He stared up at the chief slave in terror, fixed to the spot. Pete crawled out from behind the broken piece of amphora and knelt down next to Julius.

"Please, sir. It was just an accident," Pete babbled to Snottius, clasping his hands together pleadingly.

"Oh yes. Of course. Accidents *do* happen, don't they?" Snottius replied mockingly. Then he turned his head and barked, "Thuglus! Dummus! Come here now!"

It sounded like he was ordering two misbehaving dogs to come to him.

What appeared in the doorway, though, was far worse than two misbehaving dogs. Two monstrous giants lumbered into view. They bumped into each other as each of them struggled to get through the door in front of the other. Snottius rolled his eyes, put his hands on his hips, and started tapping his foot impatiently. Eventually the two of them got through the door and arrived next to Snottius.

Pete now got a proper view of them and gulped. He'd heard their names before, whispered quietly between the other slaves in terror, but had not yet met these two beasts of men. Apparently Snottius used them to keep 'badly behaved' slaves in line (well, that was the least bad rumour about what they did). They towered over Snottius. Their biceps were bigger than Pete's waist, maybe even Pete's and Julius's waists put together! They were just as ugly as they were huge.

"Yeah, boss, yeah, boss. What you want?" one of the giants asked Snottius, sounding like an excited puppy.

"Seize these two ungrateful slackers," Snottius shrieked, pointing at Pete and Julius.

Thuglus and Dummus now lumbered towards the two boys, licking their lips excitedly. They obviously enjoyed doing what Snottius asked them to do. They then bumped into each other again, each of them trying to go for Pete at the same time. They then stood back, looked at each other highly confused, and then bumped into each other again as both now went for Julius. It seemed they were just as stupid as they were huge and ugly.

Snottius lost his patience. "You blithering idiots!" he screamed. "Thuglus! You take the blond one! Dummus, you take the *other one*!" Snottius said 'the other one' with such contempt that Pete almost complained, but then realised that that probably wouldn't help.

Thuglus grabbed Julius by one arm and flung him over his shoulder. It looked like he was picking up a bag of oranges rather than a rather tall thirteen-year-old boy. Then Dummus grabbed Pete by the foot and picked him up. He looked into Pete's upside-down face and then laughed. "This one look stoopid," he chuckled to Thuglus. Pete thought that was very rich coming from Dummus, but he wasn't in a position to say anything. Dummus now threw Pete over his shoulder.

"Follow me," Snottius said with obvious delight in his voice as he walked up the steps back into the corridor.

The two goons followed their boss back to the kitchen with Julius's and Pete's bodies bouncing on their shoulders as they lurched forward.

They entered the kitchen where the other slaves were just finishing clearing up after dinner. As Dummus turned into the kitchen Pete noticed that the other slaves started working a lot more quickly.

"Leave them there!" Snottius yelled, pointing to a spot on the kitchen floor.

Thuglus and Dummus dropped their burdens on to the floor and stepped back to watch the entertainment.

Julius finally spoke. "This is all your fault, Pete," he blubbered through tears.

"Thanks for the loyalty!" Pete snarled back at him. "I was only trying to help."

"Silence!" Snottius shrieked. He then paused and turned round to the other slaves, who were giving the impression of being far too absorbed in their work to notice what was going on.

"These *boys*," Snottius began with a dismissive flick of the hand towards Pete and Julius, "think they're better than you and they shouldn't have to help you clear up after dinner."

Snottius paused as if he was expecting all the other slaves to stop and thank him or jeer at the boys. They hardly even noticed, so he continued: "Don't worry though. They *will* be punished," he said with a horrible smile twisting his lips.

He turned to where the two unfortunate boys were sitting on the floor and said with satisfaction in his voice, "It's **latrine** duty for you two."

The biggest and most sinister grin Pete had ever seen now covered Snottius's face.

"What's that?" Pete whispered to Julius.

Julius did not reply, but the horrified look on his face told Pete all that he needed to know.

The Amphora

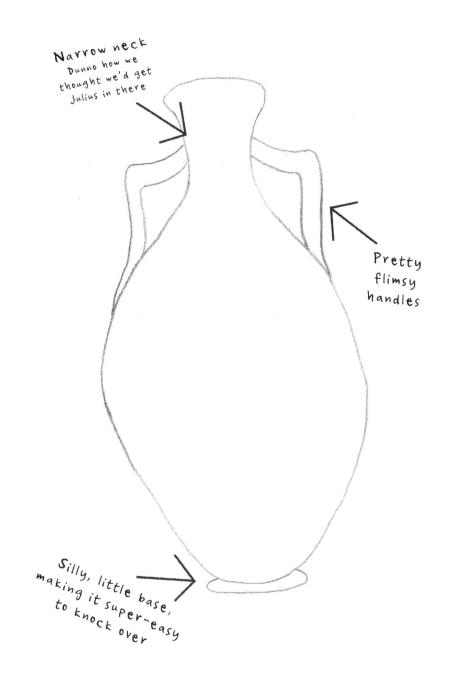

Narrow neck
Dunno how we thought we'd get Julius in there

Pretty flimsy handles

Silly, little base, making it super-easy to knock over

Chapter 22

PETE DIDN'T HAVE LONG TO wait to find out what latrine duty was. Snottius led the two boys around to a wooden building that was separate from the rest of the house. Pete could smell it before he saw it. Snottius introduced them to a very dirty and a very unhappy slave called Briacus.

"Show these two dogs how to do your job, Briacus. You will be relieved of your duties for now," Snottius explained to the unhappy slave whose face lit up at these words.

"Really?" Briacus asked excitedly. "Of course, sir. Anything you say, sir."

With that Snottius took one last satisfied look at the two boys and left.

"OK, boys. You heard Snottius," Briacus said with a smile on his face. "Follow me."

Briacus led the boys inside the wooden building, where the smell became unbearable. Pete couldn't see anything very clearly as a sort of mist hung in the air. Once his eyes readjusted he saw what looked like a bench against the wall. As his eyes adjusted further, he noticed there were four holes in the bench from which the smell seemed to be coming.

Pete realised what these must be and he also realised

that until this point, he had only been for a pee in the first century AD. It hadn't crossed his mind what he would do if he needed to do anything else.

"Well, boys, your job will be to keep these clean," Briacus explained, indicating the 'bench' with his hand. "I'll get you some shovels. Follow me."

Briacus led them out of the building and round to the back of it. Julius looked at Pete with dread on his face.

"Oh, Pete, what have you done?" Julius whined.

At the back of the building Briacus handed the boys a shovel each and said, "Let's go in."

He took them down into a pit below and behind the building. Pete couldn't hold his stomach in check any longer and was sick into a sort of stream that was running from under the building.

"You'll get used to the smell," Briacus told the boys breezily. "So, this water," he continued, pointing to the stream into which Pete had just been sick, "washes the 'stuff' from above to this end over here." Briacus led them to a very big pile of 'stuff'.

"It can't all stay here of course," Briacus explained with a chuckle, "and that's why we have the shovels. Come on, boys, get a good shovel-full of the 'stuff' and follow me."

The boys did as they were told, though very slowly. Pete held his breath as he got close to the pile to avoid being sick again. They both got about a fifth of a shovel-full and followed Briacus out of the pit and up into the fresh (or, at least, *fresher*) air. Pete was still struggling to hold his breath: he did *not* want to smell what was on his shovel.

Briacus emptied his shovel into a cart which was standing

behind the building and the boys did the same. Pete put down his shovel and started gulping in breaths of air. Briacus laughed very heartily.

"Right, boys. You just keep doing that until the cart's full. Then you pull it over to that field over there, where it will get used as fertiliser. And that's it," Briacus said, dusting his hands off with satisfaction. "Any questions?"

Julius was dumbstruck and did not utter a word. Pete was desperately trying not to be sick again and so he couldn't say a word.

"Great," Briacus said with a smile. "Well, I'll let you get on with it," he added and then walked off towards Probus's house.

The two boys looked at each other in disbelief.

"I hate you, Pete. I wish Master hadn't bought you," Julius yelled at our hero.

Pete concluded that this might be a good time to leave 'the land of the underpants'.

Chapter 23

Back in his own bedroom, Pete breathed a sigh of relief. He was pleased to be away from those latrines and not to be feeling sick anymore. He did feel guilty about Julius though. He'd got the poor boy into this very unpleasant situation. He really should get him out. In spite of this, Pete desperately didn't want to go back.

He slept very badly that night and was very distracted at school the next day by thoughts of Julius and the pile of 'pooh' into which he had literally got his friend. Still, he couldn't bring himself to go back the next evening and just went to bed. He had another restless night.

The next evening, two days since he had last been into 'the land of the underpants', Auntie Cheryl rang. Mum answered and Pete could hear her talking to her friend. After a little while, Pete heard Mum say, "What's that, Cheryl? You want to find out how Pete's getting on with his History homework?"

Mum looked over at Pete, who was watching television in the room next door and really didn't want to speak to his aunt. "He's just here. I'll pass you on to him," Mum said as she beckoned to her unwilling son to come over to the phone in the kitchen.

"Hi, Auntie Cher," Pete drawled unenthusiastically.

"How's our young time-travelling hero, then?" Auntie Cheryl asked enthusiastically.

"All right, I suppose," Pete replied slowly.

"Good. Right, can anyone hear you? I want to know how it's going with the underpants," Auntie Cheryl explained conspiratorially.

Pete looked around and saw that Mum and Dad were watching the television at full volume in the next room (Dad swore he wasn't going deaf, but the rest of the family were not so sure). Jim was out at football practice and Susie was away at university for another few weeks.

"It's OK, no one can hear," Pete responded begrudgingly.

"Well? What's going on?" Auntie Cheryl asked.

Pete explained slowly and lethargically all about Julius and the latrines. When he had finished, Auntie Cheryl took a breath and said, "You can't leave Julius like that, Pete."

"Why not?" Pete asked. "It's your fault I even went there in the first place. You go and help him."

Of course Pete knew he couldn't leave Julius in trouble like that. He had spoken more out of anger than anything else.

"Maybe you're right, Pete. But don't you want to see how this ends? Think of the other adventures you can have in other periods of history once you've completed your task with Julius," Auntie Cheryl said in a conciliatory tone, realising that Pete may have a point.

"Yeah, I guess it would be good to see how it ends and go

to some other time in history," Pete conceded, brightening a little.

"So will you do it, Pete? Will you put the time-travelling Y-fronts back on?" she asked him.

"OK," Pete replied sulkily.

"I couldn't hear you then, Pete. Say it. Say 'I will put the time-travelling underpants back on'," Auntie Cheryl prompted her godson.

"I'll put the time-travelling pants back on," Pete repeated after his aunt, a little tetchily.

"What was that? I don't believe you," Auntie Cheryl responded with a laugh.

"OK, OK. I *will* put the time-travelling pants back on," Pete said with conviction and a chuckle.

"What's that about time-travelling pants?"

Pete turned to see Dad standing at the open fridge and looking at Pete with a confused expression.

Chapter 24

"**Y**OU WHAT, DAD?" PETE SAID after a long pause which felt like an eternity. Pete realised that, during this pause, Auntie Cheryl had hung up. What a supportive godmother she was.

"I could have sworn you were saying something about wearing time-travelling pants on the phone just then," Dad replied with an amused expression.

Pete wasn't sure what to say, but the awkward silence was interrupted by Mum coming in.

"Couldn't you find the chocolate, darling?" she said as she came into the kitchen. "Oh, hello. What are you two chatting about?" she asked, noticing her husband and son facing each other.

Dad turned to Mum with a slightly bemused smile and said, "Pete was talking to Cheryl about time-travelling pants."

"What?" Mum replied with an incredulous giggle.

This had given Pete some thinking time. "No Mum, Dad misheard," he explained, "I was just talking about the underpants science experiment to Auntie Cheryl."

"But I could have sworn he said—" Dad began, pointing at his son.

But Mum interjected, "Oh, Harry, you know you're going deaf." She looked at Pete and rolled her eyes. "Don't leave the fridge door open. How many times have I told you?" she remonstrated with her husband as she took the chocolate, which he had been sent to get, out of the fridge and closed the door.

"Anyway, come on," she continued to her husband. "The ad break must be over by now."

"Huh, oh, OK," Mr Tollywash replied, still obviously unsure what to think.

The excitement of almost being caught by Dad had left Pete rather exhausted. His heart was still racing. Talking to Auntie Cheryl had got Pete excited about going back to help Julius. But the excitement had turned to panic when his father had interrupted.

He took two deep breaths and sat on the kitchen chair for a few more minutes. Then he made a decision. He *was* going to go back to help Julius, but not tonight. That narrow escape with Dad had convinced him that he was meant to do this, but that he needed to be a bit more careful about it.

"I'm really tired and I'm going to get an early night," Pete told his parents as he walked through to the lounge.

"Are you not feeling so well?" Mum asked, shocked at this odd behaviour from her son. She could not remember a time when he had voluntarily gone to bed early.

"That must be it," Pete answered, pleased to take this opportunity to allay any suspicion from his mother.

Pete walked slowly up the stairs and flopped down onto his bed. He genuinely was tired.

Chapter 25

Pete couldn't wait for school to end the next day, nor for bedtime to come. He was now very excited at the thought of going back to the first century AD.

Back in his room he took out the underpants from his wardrobe and looked at them for a few seconds. All the excitement disappeared and he suddenly felt very nervous about going back. Should he really do this? He dithered for a few moments and then remembered Julius. He couldn't leave him in the lurch. He made up his mind and put on his tunic and then the underpants. He felt his hips pull away as he was propelled back to the spot where he had left Julius.

"I've had nothing but trouble since you came," Julius continued as tears came to his eyes.

Pete remembered now how badly he had left things with Julius.

"But, it's not my fault," Pete began, but Julius put his hand up, forcing him to stop.

"Shut up, Pete! From now on I don't want to talk to you. Let's just do our work!" Julius barked back at his former friend as he picked up his shovel.

Pete decided to listen to Julius, who seemed really angry

now, and also picked up his shovel. The two of them just shovelled in silence. Julius's anger and Pete's sense of guilt kept Pete's mind off the smell. Still, it was hard, back-breaking work.

After a few hours of mind-numbing toil, Pete decided he needed something to break the monotony. He had started hankering after those dormice dipped in honey which he had so enjoyed. He began to have little daydreams about eating them. Before long, he couldn't satisfy himself with daydreams. When Briacus came to tell them they were done for the day, Pete decided he had to act. He had to find the dormice.

The kitchen was empty when Pete arrived as it was so late and everyone had finished for the day. He started looking around in various pots and jars, but it seemed the dormice were well hidden (well they were a delicacy and slaves weren't meant to have them). He thrust his hand into cupboard after cupboard and opened pot and jar after pot and jar. He took out one very large and very heavy jar and took off the lid. He gave a little squeal and almost dropped it when he saw what was inside. It was dormice, all right. But these dormice were still alive! He quickly put the lid back on and replaced the jar in the cupboard. Our hero had inadvertently picked up a *glirarium*: a jar in which live dormice were fattened up ready for eating.

Pete slumped down onto a stool.

Caradocus came into the kitchen and startled Pete.

"Oh, Pete, what are you doing here?" the cook asked with surprise.

Pete leapt up from his stool and took a step back towards the stove. He bumped into it and a wooden panel fell open.

"Oh careful, Pete," Caradocus said as he rushed over to replace the panel. Before the cook could replace the panel, though, Pete caught a glimpse of the unmistakable sight of honey-glazed dormice.

These ones definitely were not alive.

Chapter 26

PETE ACTED VERY CASUALLY AS if he hadn't seen the dormice. In the confusion Caradocus forgot to ask again why Pete was there. Pete bid Caradocus 'good night' and went off to dream of delicious dormice covered in honey (and forget the unfortunate living dormice in the *glirarium*).

Pete made the most of his discovery over the next couple of days, sneaking a dormouse whenever he could. He had to be careful not to take too many in case Caradocus noticed the dwindling supply of rodents. This only very partially made up for the disgusting task that he and Julius had been set. The only plus-side to the very smelly task was that it covered up the fact that eating the dormice had started to give Pete wind.

After two days on latrine duty and with no indication of when they would, if ever, be relieved from it, Pete decided something needed to be done. He didn't want to spend the rest of his days shovelling pooh. He was desperate to free Julius and then see what his next adventure might be. The only problem was that Julius was still not talking to Pete and so it was impossible to discuss any sort of escape plan. So, as someone once said, desperate times called for desperate measures.

On the third day of latrine duty, Snottius came to gloat over, sorry, *inspect* Pete's and Julius's work.

"Having fun, boys?" Snottius asked with a malicious smile on his cruel lips.

The two boys ignored him and continued shovelling.

"Hey! Answer your superior when he speaks to you!" Snottius barked.

"Yes, sir," the two boys groaned in unison.

"That'll teach you *snivelling* rats to shirk your duties ... *and* break an amphora that's worth far more than the two of you put together," Snottius sneered.

Pete and Julius just groaned, "Yes, sir," again.

Snottius chuckled malevolently to himself and walked over towards the pit where the boys were working. He bent over and peered in at the revolting pile.

"Pee-yoo," he said, holding his nose dramatically. "I'm not sure what smells worse. The pile or *you two.*" Snottius stood up next to the pit and rocked himself with laughter at his wonderful little joke.

Pete walked past with a full shovel and then thought he saw his opportunity. As he returned to the pit with his empty shovel he 'bumped' into Snottius.

"Oops. What a clumsy boy I am!" Pete said as he watched Snottius tumble head over heels into the pit. As Snottius landed head first right in the middle of the pile, Pete turned to Julius and cried, "Run!"

Just as it had succeeded with the man in the tip when Pete was looking for the underpants, shouting 'Run' confused

Julius and he obeyed without thinking. He followed Pete and quickly overtook him. Pete turned to see Snottius struggling out of the pit, only to slip over and fall back in.

"Quick, in here!" Julius said as they arrived at a barn on the edge of Probus's estate.

Once they were in and hiding behind some hay, Julius whispered to Pete, "You stupid clumsy oaf." Then there was a silence and Pete could then hear Julius sobbing quietly to himself.

"Why did I run?" Julius moaned. "Now I'll be in even more trouble. I should have just stayed and let *you* get in trouble," he continued, turning to Pete. "*You* pushed Snottius in. It's *your* problem."

"But wait," Pete said, "we got away didn't we? It'll take 'em ages to find us here. There's so many barns and hiding places on Probus's estate. If we wait here till night, then we can escape properly."

Julius calmed down a little at this. "Well, if I go back now, I'll just be in trouble anyway, so I suppose I'd better give it a go then," he said begrudgingly to Pete.

"There you go. We'll make it out. Don't worry," Pete reassured Julius.

Julius remained silent and Pete got the impression that he was not speaking to him again.

Time dragged by and the boys stayed in their hiding-place in silence. Pete started to get hungry and then remembered that he had a stolen dormouse still in his pocket which he hadn't had a chance to eat earlier. He tried to sneak mouthfuls of it without Julius noticing. He didn't want to share this tasty morsel.

"What are you eating?" Julius asked. He had noticed chewing noises coming from Pete through the silence of the barn.

Pete was desperate to keep every bit for himself, so he thought quickly. "Hay," he lied back to the other boy.

"You really are an animal," Julius replied, shaking his head in disgust.

"Yeah, I guess so," Pete agreed with a grin.

An animal with a belly-full of tasty dormouse though, he thought smugly to himself.

Their conversation was interrupted by voices outside. The unmistakable nasal whine of Snottius was amongst them.

The owners of the voices came into the barn and the two boys held their breaths. This was probably a bad idea for Pete. His dormouse had had the usual effect and he was feeling rather gassy. He tried to contain himself, but it was no use. Just as Snottius and his gang were about to leave, an almighty sound broke the silence.

"That doesn't sound like a horse," Snottius could be heard to say as he and his gang made their way towards the place from where the noise had come.

Thuglus...or is it
Dummus?

Wonky
eyes

Awful
hair

Huge
Muscles

Disgusting
teeth

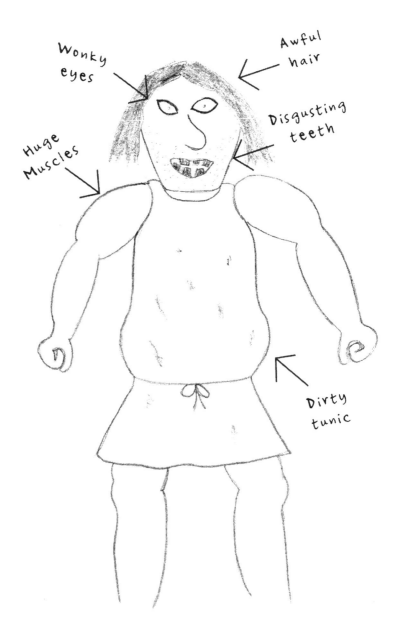

Dirty
tunic

Chapter 27

THE RECOGNISABLE SMELL OF THE latrine pit got stronger and stronger as Snottius made his way towards the boys' hiding-place. He put his hand into the pile of hay in which they were hiding and touched Julius's head. Julius squeaked and then covered his mouth, but it was too late. Snottius brushed the straw back.

A very dirty face with a huge hooked nose appeared before the boys. He had managed to remove most of the unpleasant stuff into which he had fallen, but Snottius was still pretty filthy and very smelly.

"A-ha. It's our little runaways. I've found the little dormouse droppings," he said, turning to Thuglus and Dummus.

The two giants lumbered over and picked the boys out of the hay.

"Hey boss, these two smell almost as bad as you," Thuglus said to Snottius and started laughing, but Snottius did not laugh.

Snottius clipped Thuglus round the ear and asked him, "Do you want to join them on latrine duty?"

Thuglus lifted his hand to his ear to rub it. Unfortunately, it was the hand with which he was holding Pete and our unfortunate hero fell like a sack of potatoes to the floor. Understandably, he started crying, which set poor Julius off too.

"It's no good, you little toe-rags," Snottius jeered. "Tears won't save two little runaway slaves."

"But it was an accident, sir," Pete snivelled through his tears and snot.

"Why did you run away, then?" Snottius countered.

"We ran because we were scared, sir," Julius interjected. "We just got confused. We were already in trouble and were scared of getting in more trouble. It was just an accident."

"Whatever," Snottius scoffed. "Bring them back to the house," he then ordered Thuglus and Dummus.

As he walked ahead of them, Snottius snorted and muttered to himself. "Horrible Brittunculi. No respect for their betters. No better than animals."

He then turned towards the two giants and the two small boys and a sinister smile covered his face. It was made all the more gruesome by the fact that it was still pretty well covered in nasty stuff. "We'll see what Master Probus has to say about this. Escaped slaves don't tend to get very nice treatment," he said as he rubbed his hands together.

Thuglus complained bitterly all the way to the house. "This little ratbag keeps blowing off. It stinks," he kept saying.

The dormouse was still having its effect on Pete, it seemed.

They arrived at the house and Thuglus and Dummus dumped the two boys in the granary where Pete had learned to separate wheat from chaff. Snottius left them to go to speak with Probus.

"Huh, huh, huh," Dummus guffawed. "Them two's in for it. Never seen the boss so angry."

"Yeah! And that's saying something," Thuglus sniggered in agreement.

"Maybe he'll let us have our fun," Dummus said, his eyes brightening as he spoke.

"Ah, yeah," Thuglus replied with a broad smile. "Not done any proper bone-crushing in aaaaages!"

Dummus chuckled with glee. "We always get to do our best work with runaway slaves."

Pete and Julius swallowed hard as they remembered the rumours about Thuglus and Dummus.

"Wonder if those two will survive long enough to admire our handiwork?" Thuglus asked his partner-in-crime.

The two man-mountains shook with laughter as they looked at the terrified boys cowering before them.

Chapter 28

A VERY ANGRY SNOTTIUS RETURNED TO the granary. "Why did no one stop me going to speak to Probus with *this* still all over me?" he asked, pointing to the 'stuff' on his face and most of his body. "Anyway," he continued angrily, "we have to go and see Master Probus."

Thuglus and Dummus picked the boys up again. They took them through to a room which Pete hadn't been in before. It was very large with cushions and chairs around the edge and paintings on the walls, just like the room in which he had been interviewed by Noxius Maximus. Probus was sitting at the end of the room on a large chair on a raised stage. This place was far grander than any of the rooms Pete had so far seen.

"Ah, there's my prize purchase," he said on seeing Pete and laughed at his own joke. "Snottius has told me all about your amusing little adventures. That's just the reason why I bought you. Liven this place up a bit."

Snottius began, "But Master, I must protest—"

"—Must you protest, really, Snottius?" Probus interrupted him. "It is most tiresome when you do."

After speaking to his chief slave, Probus then turned

and looked at Julius and Pete, still with a smile on his face. "Anyway, I suppose you must be punished for what you did to Snottius, even though you've given me a very good giggle..."

He paused, deep in thought.

Julius and Pete stared at their master in terror, awaiting the terrible torture they would receive at the hands of Thuglus and Dummus.

After a while longer, Probus said, "How about two days serving Master Superbus?"

"What?" Snottius bellowed. "That's not a punishment!"

"Snottius, you've met my son," Probus replied in a very superior tone. "Two days working exclusively for him is enough punishment for most crimes. Please don't question my judgements. Oh, and next time, please wash before coming to see me. All dismissed," Probus concluded, waving his hands at them to shoo them away.

With that, Dummus and Thuglus carried the rather fortunate boys out of the room and Snottius followed behind. Pete could hear Snottius snorting and muttering to himself.

When Julius and Pete were alone again they breathed a sigh of relief. Having to work for their master's son (or 'snot-for-brains') would be a pain, but it would be a lot better than latrine duty.

"He's actually quite nice, you know, Probus," said Julius. "For a slave-master, that is."

"If he was that nice he'd let us all go," Pete replied incredulously.

Julius looked very surprised at this. It seemed the thought had never crossed his mind.

"But how would he run his estate then?" Julius asked Pete.

"He could just pay people to work for him," Pete responded, shocked at how stupid Julius was being.

"Pay people to work for you?" Julius said, slightly confused.

Pete could see he wasn't following him, so he changed the subject. "Hey, we'll be working with Superbus all day, so that gives us plenty of time to play tricks on him. You told me you liked doing that," Pete said, suddenly realising that this punishment may not only be better than latrine duty, but it might actually be fun.

"Oh no, Pete. You've already got me into enough trouble," Julius replied with conviction.

"But we got away with it," Pete reasoned, surprised that Julius was still cross with him. However, he could see from Julius's face that he was far from forgiving him.

Chapter 29

I N SPITE OF JULIUS'S REFUSAL to join in, Pete could not resist playing tricks on Superbus. Probus's son had the 'attractive' combination of arrogance and stupidity, so to Pete it seemed that he was only getting what he deserved.

At first though, it very much seemed that the joke was on Pete, as he had to wash Superbus's underwear or *subligacula* as everyone else called it. Washing Superbus's underwear was bad enough, but that wasn't the worst part.

"Ugh, what's that?" Pete asked as he watched Julius pour out the washing liquid.

"It's for washing the clothes, of course," Julius replied with confusion all over his face.

"But it stinks!" Pete complained, holding his nose.

"Well, duh. Pee smells doesn't it?" Julius replied impatiently.

"Yeah, I guess it does … What? Pee?"

Julius's words took a while to sink in with Pete.

"What else are we going to wash these in?" Julius asked.

"Well, Ariel, like Mum uses," Pete replied.

Julius looked up with interest. "What's Ariel? I thought you didn't have a mum, Pete?"

Pete remembered where he was and the fact that he'd told Julius he didn't know where his parents were. "Oh, it's nothing. Was just a thought. I did have a mum, of course, but I dunno where she is now."

"I miss my mum too, Pete. I hate these Romans," Julius replied forcefully. Pete's mention of a missing mother had made Julius forget about 'Ariel'.

"We need to get this washing done, Pete. Come on," Julius said as he stepped into the large bowl in which he'd put Superbus's underwear. Oh, *and* the pee.

"What? Get in there with the *pee*?" Pete asked, incredulous at Julius's suggestion.

"Yeah! Well there is *water* mixed with the pee too. Haven't you washed clothes before?" Julius asked as he started to step up and down on the clothes.

Pete thought that his recent attempt to clean his school trousers probably didn't count. He just shrugged and got in too. It didn't smell very good, but Pete was beginning to realise that nothing did in Roman times.

Later, as they were preparing for dinner, Caradocus offered Pete the perfect opportunity to prank Superbus. As they helped put together Superbus's dishes, Caradocus interrupted.

"Woah, boys. You can't put that in there," Caradocus cried, pointing to a radish that Julius was about to put into Superbus's dish. "He's really allergic to them. If he so much as smells a radish he comes out in a really bad rash which makes him itchy for days," Caradocus added with a chuckle, clearly amused by a memory of the last time Superbus had radish.

Pete smiled a wicked smile to himself at this wonderful piece of news.

The next time the boys had to wash Superbus's clothes, Pete put his plan into action. He had sneaked a radish out of the kitchen while Caradocus wasn't looking. As Superbus's clothes were drying, Julius left Pete to go to the toilet. Alone now, Pete went over to the washing line and took out the radish. He bit off a chunk and spat it straight out. He hated all vegetables, but raw radish was perhaps the worst of the lot, he thought. He then went along the washing line, rubbing the radish all over Superbus's underpants.

Next day Probus was holding a *salutatio*. Julius explained to Pete that quite a few other Romans and some Britons living locally relied on Probus for money and favours.

"What? So Probus gives these people money?" Pete asked.

"Yes. These people are his clients," Julius explained. "Probus gives them money and helps them out if they have trouble. In return, they help Probus in whatever way he asks them to."

"Right. So what's this *salutatio* then?" Pete asked.

"Oh, it's just one of these silly Roman things they like to do. The clients have to come to pay Probus their respects. In return, Probus hands out money to them."

Pete liked the sound of this, but thought that if he tried going up to his neighbours in Guildford to ask for money, they'd probably chase him off their doorstep with a cricket bat.

Julius and Pete came to the *salutatio* to serve Superbus. Superbus had pride of place next to this father. Pete's and Julius's job was to hand little baskets with money in them to Superbus.

Partway through the ceremony Superbus suddenly started playing with his toga and fidgeting around in his seat. He was starting to feel the effects of the radish. His father Probus was muttering to him under his breath things like, "Stop embarrassing me," and, "I knew it was too soon to let you meet the clients."

Then Superbus could bear the discomfort no longer and leapt up from his seat, throwing the basket Pete had just handed to him on to the floor. Everyone then stood up, looking at Superbus with open mouths (including Pete, trying to act surprised) as he then started *taking off his toga*.

Probus was livid by this point and began shouting at his son to leave, but Superbus was too busy trying to take his clothes off to notice. He started taking off his tunic and was then standing in the middle of the room in only his underpants.

Fortunately, he realised where he was before he took these off too!

Superbus

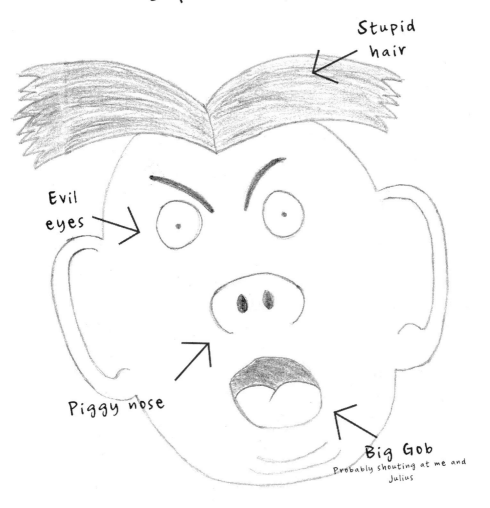

Stupid hair

Evil eyes

Piggy nose

Big Gob
Probably shouting at me and Julius

Chapter 30

SUPERBUS STOOD FOR A GOOD minute looking around the room at all the shocked faces. Then he felt the itch again and started jumping around like he was on fire and scratching his bottom.

"Everyone is dismissed!" Probus yelled.

Probus's clients started to leave, but a few left very slowly, watching Superbus over their shoulders and trying not to laugh.

Probus grabbed his son by the hand (the hand with which he was scratching his bottom).

"What on earth do you think you are doing?" Probus asked his son, who was just as surprised as Probus was at this strange turn of events.

"I-I-I I can't help it, Dad!" Superbus whined. "It's *really* itchy!"

"I bet it is! You always think you're funny, don't you?" Probus replied angrily.

"But-but-but, it's not my fault. I bet *they* did it!" Superbus cried, pointing at Julius and Pete, who were standing obediently by, trying hard not to laugh.

Julius and Pete stared back with innocence all over their

faces (which was fair enough for Julius—he had had nothing to do with it).

"What? *They* embarrassed me? *They* hopped around like a baboon and took all their clothes off, did they? You can never take the blame, can you?" Probus concluded, turning and walking away from his son.

Superbus burst into tears and began scratching his bottom again. "I bet it *was* you!" he whimpered through his tears as he turned to Pete and Julius.

The two other boys stayed silent. They were meant to, just like good slaves.

Superbus yelled at them, "You heard my father. Everyone is dismissed!" and he limped off to his room, still scratching his bottom and muttering.

Pete was very pleased with the success of his prank, but, if he was honest, he also felt a little sorry for Superbus and a little guilty. He hadn't quite meant to humiliate him as badly as he had. Only a little guilty, it has to be said, as Superbus still continued to behave in his usual, insufferably arrogant way.

However, Pete served Superbus like a perfect Roman slave for the next two days. This further convinced Probus that Superbus had been lying when he blamed the boys for his impromptu dancing performance at the *salutatio*. It also had the added benefit of convincing Probus to end their punishment and let them return to working for Caradocus and on the farm.

After a few days back at the old tasks, Pete realised he preferred working for Superbus. If you ignored the fact that he was a complete rat-faced little weasel, then you could have quite a bit of fun.

Julius had got bored of giving Pete the silent treatment and began talking to him again. After a little while he had forgotten that he had been angry with Pete at all and returned to telling him about Boudicca. Of course, they had to wait till times when they were on their own. If they had been overheard talking about a rebel queen, then Probus might not have decided to save them from the grips of Thuglus and Dummus.

"My Aunt Boudicca was queen around here before I was born," Julius whispered to Pete one night before they went to sleep. "My uncle, her husband, made friends with the Romans when they invaded so that they wouldn't take his land. They let him stay as king as long as he was loyal to the Romans."

"What, so he was king, but the Romans were, like, in charge, you mean?" Pete asked.

"Kind of. But he died and the Romans just came and took over the land," Julius continued in a whisper.

"What? So they took the land off your aunt?" Pete asked.

"Yeah. I don't know loads about what happened then, 'cause it was before I was born," Julius explained. "But later, when the Romans were invading somewhere else, Aunt Boudicca decided she would use the opportunity to fight back."

"Good for her!" Pete almost shouted, but then quickly quietened down so as not to wake anyone.

"Keep it down, Pete," Julius warned him and then continued. "She marched to Camulodunum and *flattened* it," Julius explained with satisfaction.

"Oh, that's where I was in prison," Pete interrupted.

"What?" Julius replied.

"Oh, nothing. Go on. Go on," Pete encouraged his friend.

"Oh, OK. Then Boudicca marched on a place called Londinium," Julius continued enthusiastically.

"London?" Pete interrupted in confusion.

"What? Stop interrupting, Pete," Julius admonished him, more interested in telling the story than what this strange word 'London', which Pete had uttered, meant.

"My dad was with his big sister Boudicca and he told me they burnt it down and killed most of the people," Julius continued with bloodthirsty glee.

"What?" Pete interrupted. "That's not very nice. Did she need to kill all those people?" Pete asked.

"They deserved it, Pete," Julius explained as if it were obvious.

"Oh, OK," Pete replied, less sure than his friend.

"Anyway, then my aunt went to Verulamium," Julius continued, ignoring Pete.

"Very-lame-ium?" Pete interrupted in amusement, forgetting the poor people of Londinium.

"Stop interrupting, Pete!" Julius was now losing his patience. "Anyway, of course she flattened that place as well," Julius said with satisfaction.

Pete had realised by now that Boudicca wasn't to be messed with.

"Unfortunately the Roman soldiers who'd been fighting

somewhere else were now back and itching for a fight with my aunt," Julius said with a sigh. "But my aunt was a great warrior," he added, suddenly brightening, "and she led my dad and the rest of her army against those Romans."

"And then what?" Pete asked excitedly.

"You must know how it ended, Pete? Would I be a slave here if my aunt had won?" Julius asked in disbelief at his friend's stupidity.

"Oh, I guess not," Pete replied with disappointment in his voice.

Chapter 31

THINGS SETTLED INTO A ROUTINE again and Pete quickly got used to it. You just do, don't you? Even if that routine is flashing back and forth between the twenty-first and first centuries! Pete didn't ask Julius any more about Boudicca (even though he wanted to). He sensed that Julius was very happy to talk about the rebellion, but not about how it ended or what happened afterwards.

Pete complained to Auntie Cheryl one evening, as he was starting to get a little bored again.

"I don't know how I'm ever going to free Julius," Pete sighed down the telephone receiver.

"Now, Pete, chin up," Auntie Cheryl encouraged her godson. "Opportunities present themselves when you least expect it."

"Well they haven't done yet," Pete whined. "They're watching us like hawks after we tried to escape."

"Just keep your eyes peeled, my boy. I often found things had a habit of working themselves out when I used to do the old time-travelling bit," Auntie Cheryl advised Pete, rather uselessly, Pete thought.

"In fact," Auntie Cheryl continued, "I remember one

particular adventure where it seemed like it would never end, but suddenly the solution dropped into my lap."

"How long was that, Auntie Cher?" Pete asked with interest and trepidation.

"Oh, that was my Egyptian adventure. Probably took me about six months that one," Auntie Cheryl answered casually.

"Six months?" Pete groaned, too disheartened by this revelation to show any interest in what this 'Egyptian adventure' might have been.

That evening, once Pete had donned the famous underpants and been whisked back to Roman East Anglia, Caradocus came with some news.

"Now boys, you've been serving me so well since that little 'incident'," Caradocus began, with a little chuckle as he referred to Snottius's run-in with the pile of pooh, "that I've convinced Snottius that you can help me with shopping."

He looked at the two boys, waiting for a reaction, but all they did was nod, rather underwhelmed by the news.

Slightly deflated at the boys' lack of enthusiasm, Caradocus continued: "It does mean you'll be leaving the estate a number of times a week. I thought you'd be pleased," he said with obvious disappointment in his voice.

At this clarification from Caradocus, the boys brightened a little. They hadn't really left the house since they'd been caught in the barn.

"Anyway, I said I'd convinced Snottius to let you join me to do the shopping. He only agreed on the understanding that if you two got up to *any mischief*, I'd be punished too,"

Caradocus added with a very serious face and looking both boys in the eye, one-by-one.

Pete took this as the cue to speak. "We won't let you down, Caradocus," Pete reassured the cook with an encouraging smile. "Isn't that right, Julius?"

"No, no, we won't let you down," Julius agreed with slightly less gusto.

What had Auntie Cheryl said to Pete about opportunities coming when you least expected it?

After Caradocus had left the boys chopping vegetables, Pete whispered to Julius, "Now's our chance. We can escape when we're out with Caradocus."

Julius put down his knife and turned face-on to Pete. He whispered through gritted teeth almost in a snarl, "Now, look, *Pete*. I'm not getting into any more trouble over your stupid schemes." So saying, Julius waggled a menacing finger in Pete's face.

"But what about your aunt? What about the spirit of Boudicca's rebellion?" Pete replied with hurt in his voice.

"That was a long time ago and it didn't work," Julius corrected Pete. "Anyway, you heard Caradocus. If we cause any trouble, he'll get punished too. Do you want that? *Really?*"

"No, I guess not," Pete responded with a heavy sigh.

"Good. Just chop your carrots and stop trying to get us all punished ... or *worse*," Julius advised Pete with a sinister look on his face.

Or worse? Uh oh.

Pete swallowed hard and returned to his chopping. Obviously Auntie Cheryl had no idea what she was talking about.

Chapter 32

THE MARKET IN CAMULODUNUM WAS a bit of a shock for Pete. Not that it should have been after all the time he had now spent in Roman Britain. He had expected it to be like going to the MegaMart, which his family all went to on Saturday mornings. Obviously he didn't expect there to be a huge car park and gigantic aircraft hangar-sized supermarket (he understood that much about the Roman age now). But he hadn't expected the fact that each different type of food was sold by a different shop. *What a hassle!* And he most certainly didn't expect the smell (even after his latrine duty!).

They went round from stall to stall with Caradocus as he bought what he needed and explained everything to the boys. They arrived at the first shop (well it wasn't really a shop, more a pile of vegetables with a man standing by them). Caradocus made his order, paid the man and gave the vegetables to the boys to carry.

Then they moved on to another area of the market, turning into a street of low buildings. This was where the smell got really bad. Pete could see a row of buildings with big shelves sticking out of them either side of the street. As he walked past the first one he let out a scream. There was something large and covered in blood inside the building.

"What is it, Pete?" Caradocus asked with concern.

"W-w-w-what's that?" Pete blubbered, pointing at a bloody carcass hanging from the ceiling.

"It's a sheep," Caradocus explained, perplexed by Pete's question. "I'm giving master lamb stew tonight," he continued, rubbing his hands together with delight. "That looks perfect," he added, licking his lips and looking at what Pete now knew was a dead sheep.

Pete wasn't so sure it looked perfect. He preferred the plastic-wrapped lamb chops that Mum bought.

Caradocus made his order and a very large man covered in blood picked up a huge cleaver and walked towards the sheep. Pete watched in horror as he chopped bits of the carcass and flung them on the shelf that was sticking out of the side of the building (by now Pete had realised that this shelf was actually part of the wall that swung down to make a shop counter). Caradocus wrapped the meat in cloth and handed it to Pete.

"Errrrr!" Pete moaned as Caradocus placed the meat in his hands.

Caradocus laughed and said, "You're a delicate one, aren't you, Pete? You're almost as bad as Superbus."

Pete did not like this comment and took it as the insult it was. He vowed to himself not to utter another squeal throughout the rest of the shopping trip.

"Now, boys. I have one more errand to run before we go back," Caradocus explained with a twinkle in his eye as he led the boys to a building where singing and loud laughs could be heard. They stepped in and, although it looked 2,000 years old, Pete recognised straight away what it was. There were men sitting at a table nearby rolling dice and cheering. Others were deep in conversation. Pete noticed some graffiti on the wall saying: *Servius was here, Briacus is a blockhead,* and *Don't eat here if you value your life.*

Pete was amused to find that graffiti hadn't changed much in 2,000 years.

"Are we allowed in here?" Pete whispered as he nudged Julius.

"What do you mean?" Julius asked with a blank expression on his face.

"Well, I mean, it's a pub," Pete explained. "And we're only *thirteen*," he added to clarify things.

This didn't clarify things at all for poor Julius. "Oh Pete, you are weird," he said with a shake of his head and followed Caradocus over to a table.

A man at the table stood up and cried, "Caradocus! Great to see you, you old dog! It's been a while!" as he grabbed the cook by the hand and shook it very hard.

"You too, Iolus. It's been *months*," Caradocus agreed heartily with this man they'd just met.

The other man, Iolus, disappeared and Caradocus turned to the two boys. "Of course, Snottius doesn't hear about this little errand, hey?" he said with a wink and tapping his nose.

Pete and Julius smiled at each other, trying not to laugh.

Pete spotted Iolus at a bar ladling something out of a hole into bowls and then something else out of another hole into some cups. Iolus returned with a tray with two large metal cups in the centre and two small metal cups and two bowls either side. He put the two large cups in front of Caradocus and his own empty chair and the two small cups in front of the boys. He then placed the bowls in front of the boys and said, "You must be hungry, youngsters."

Pete looked at Julius quizzically. The drink smelt rather bad, like a worse version of the beers his dad liked to drink. The bowl of food smelt even worse.

"Are we meant to drink this?" Pete asked, pointing to the cup in front of him.

"Well, duh," Julius replied, rolling his eyes. "What do you think?"

Pete took a sip and spat the drink straight back out in an arc of spray.

Caradocus and his friend started laughing at Pete and Julius joined in.

"Who's this odd little character?" Iolus asked with a grin and indicated Pete with a nod of his head.

"That's Pete," Caradocus replied, picking up his beer and attacking it with glee. "One of the slave-boys from Probus's place," he added after drinking a long draught of the stinking brew.

"And who's this young man?" Iolus asked, turning to Julius. He stopped suddenly, as if he'd been interrupted and stared long and hard at Julius.

"That's another one of them. His name's Julius," Caradocus explained with more attention on his beer than on his friend's questions.

"Julius?" Iolus asked in surprise. "Strange name for a Briton."

"Yeah, I s'pose so," Caradocus agreed with almost no interest at all. "Anyway, how have you been keeping, Iolus?"

The two friends began chattering animatedly and the boys sat there in silence. Every so often Iolus would throw a glance at Julius.

"I don't like the way he's looking at me, Pete," Julius whispered to his friend.

"It's a bit weird, isn't it?" Pete agreed, though he was referring more to the bowl of nondescript food in front of him. He remembered the graffiti warning him not to eat the food if he valued his life.

Presently, Caradocus excused himself. "Nature calls, you know," he explained with a wink.

Once he had gone, Iolus turned to Julius and looked him fully in the face.

"Caratacus? Is that you?" he asked.

Chapter 33

JULIUS LOOKED STARTLED. HE DIDN'T say a word.

"Go on, tell him," Pete said to his friend, giving him an encouraging nudge. Julius remained silent.

Pete couldn't wait any longer and spoke on his friend's behalf. "That's right," he said, with pride in his voice.

"It's so long since I saw your father, Lugobelenus," Iolus said with wonder in his voice. "You look just like him," he added, shaking his head in disbelief.

"You knew my father?" Julius asked, suddenly breaking his silence.

"Knew him? We were best friends until—" Iolus broke off abruptly and looked down. "I never saw him again," he continued, omitting to explain what it was that had ended their friendship. "You were just a baby when I last saw you," Iolus said with a smile. He then stopped as he noticed Caradocus returning. He said hurriedly in a whisper, "Come back here tomorrow. I have something of yours."

Then Caradocus arrived back at the table. "What are you all chatting about, then?" he asked with a grin.

"I was just asking the boys what that buffoon Snottius had been up to lately," Iolus replied with a wink at the boys.

"Don't get me started on *that moron*," Caradocus replied as he sat down at the table. He then proceeded to tell the tale of Snottius's encounter with the latrine pit.

By the time they left the tavern, Caradocus was rather merry. "Oh Iolus, you're my besht mate, you are," he slurred as he hugged the other man.

Iolus rolled his eyes at the boys over his friend's shoulder.

"Look after yourself, Caradocus," Iolus replied, tapping him on the back. He then turned to Julius and Pete as Caradocus started stumbling toward the door and said, "Don't forget. Be here tomorrow." Before the boys could respond, he turned and walked away.

Caradocus sat in the back of the cart and said, "Julius, you'd better drive. Caradocus needs a bit of a nap."

Julius drove the cart home while Caradocus snored loudly in the back.

"Well, how are we going to go back tomorrow, then?" Pete whispered to Julius, being careful not to wake the snoozing cook.

"We're not, Pete," Julius replied matter-of-factly.

"But this is incredible!" Pete cried. "He knows who you are. Don't you want to know more?"

"Shh. You'll wake Caradocus, *idiot*," Julius snarled back at Pete.

"But we have to know more!" Pete whined.

"Too bad," Julius said curtly. "We've got no reason to go to town."

Pete slumped down next to Caradocus in the back of the cart. Julius was right. They couldn't just run away again and Julius certainly wouldn't agree to doing that anyway.

When they got back to the house, they woke Caradocus. He stumbled out of the cart and into the kitchen. The boys followed with the shopping.

"You're drunk, you beast!" Snottius cried shrilly as he watched Caradocus wheeling about and trying to steady himself.

"And you're ugly and smelly!" Caradocus replied, feeling around for a piece of furniture to rest against.

"What did you say?" Snottius barked back at the cook. He then realised he wasn't going to get an answer as Caradocus was now too busy trying to talk to his own reflection in a pan that was hanging up.

"Why, you're a handsome devil, aren't you?" he was complimenting this other man he could see in the pan.

"What a surprise," Snottius said, turning to the boys who had appeared behind the cook. "You're not the ones making trouble this time. Anyway, get dinner ready, now! Master cannot be kept waiting," he warned them all and then walked out of the kitchen.

Making dinner was an interesting affair as Caradocus could hardly stand, let alone prepare a meal. For the most part, Caradocus just slurred instructions while sitting on a stool. Every time he did try to do anything, he almost set himself on fire or chopped his hand off, so the boys would quickly have to grab him and guide him back to his stool.

"Fetch the kidneys!" Caradocus yelled.

Julius went and got the meat pack which Pete had been given at the market. He opened it and pulled out two red squishy things and handed one to Pete. Pete held the kidney in his hand and stared at it in horror.

Caradocus was rocking on his stool with laughter. "It ain't going to hurt you, lad," he cried at Pete. "Now grab a knife and slice them open."

Pete watched as Julius slit the kidney so that it opened up like a book. He passed the knife to Pete. "Your turn. Hurry up," he said.

"Now get the pepper corns and fennel," Caradocus yelled. Julius scampered off to the storeroom where the two of them slept, while Pete very slowly cut open the kidney he had been given. He was trying hard not to be sick.

Julius returned with the ingredients he had been asked to get by Caradocus.

"Grind up the fennel and pepper and stuff them in the kidneys," Caradocus ordered as he swayed on his stool. Julius got cracking while Pete watched in dismay.

Julius filled one of the kidneys with the mixture and then tied it with a piece of string. He then passed the mixture to Pete and said, "Go on, then."

Pete very slowly obeyed and as soon as he was done, Julius put both the kidneys into a frying pan.

Preparation of the rest of the meal (sweet cheese balls as a starter, kidneys and then lamb stew) continued in a similar vein. Pete really had to work hard to contain his disgust when

Julius asked him to pass the *garum* to be added to the pear pudding.

"What?" Pete asked in shock. "You mean that fish-sauce stuff?"

"Yes. The *garum*," Julius replied matter-of-factly.

Pete then watched in dismay as Julius poured the pungent fish sauce into the ingredients for the dessert.

Fish in a pudding? These Romans really were crazy, Pete thought.

The next morning, the boys were awoken by loud groans from the room next door.

"Oh my head. What was I thinking?" Caradocus moaned.

Snottius came into the room in which the boys had been sleeping and said, "Right. You'll have to do *his* errands in town today," as he motioned towards Caradocus's room with his head. "We're all so busy preparing for the visit from the tax inspector that no one else can be spared," Snottius explained.

The boys turned and looked at each other in confusion.

"Get up! Get dressed and stop gawking like the morons you are!" Snottius yelled at the boys.

As the chief slave left, Pete noticed that he was wearing socks underneath his sandals. They had obviously been made to be worn with sandals—they even went inwards in the middle to allow the leather thong to go between the toes.

Socks with sandals? Pete thought to himself. *Obviously a loser is the same whatever period of history you're in.*

"That's great!" Julius exclaimed as he turned to Pete.

"Really?" Pete asked in disbelief. "I think socks with sandals looks awful!"

"Not Snottius's socks, you prune!" Julius cried in exasperation. "We can go to town today!"

"Oh, yeeahhh," Pete replied as it dawned on him that they might get to see Iolus again after all.

Snottius in socks and sandals

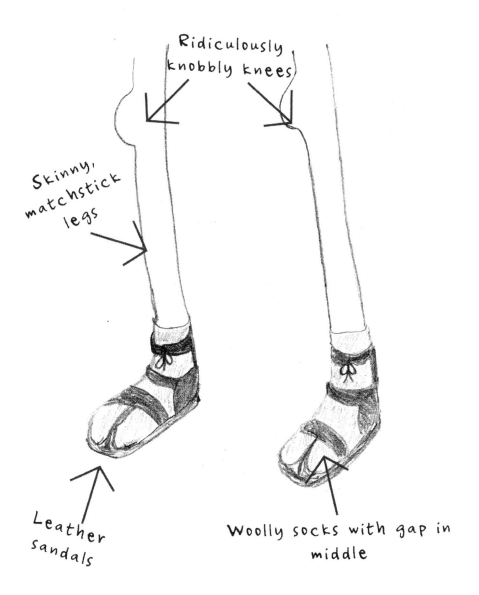

Ridiculously knobbly knees

Skinny, matchstick legs

Leather sandals

Woolly socks with gap in middle

Chapter 34

NOTTIUS RETURNED A FEW MOMENTS later to explain what
they needed to buy. Apparently Probus was going to be
entertaining the local tax inspector as he was touring the area
to calculate what everyone's taxes should be. There was going
to be a special banquet.

"Right, you better listen carefully, you little ratbags. If
you forget anything, I'll have your guts for garters," Snottius
began, waggling his finger menacingly at the boys. "So, we
need thirty oysters."

Pete grimaced as Snottius said the word 'oysters'. *Can
these Romans get any grosser?* he thought to himself.

"We need a whole congius of garum," the chief slave
continued.

I was wrong, thought Pete as he heard Snottius requesting
such a large volume of the revolting fish sauce, *these Romans
can get grosser.*

"Oi! Moron! Are you listening?"

Snottius's barking woke Pete from his thoughts.

"Yes, sir."

"So, what are the first two items then?" Snottius asked

in a sneering way that reminded Pete of Mr Briggs, his Computing teacher.

"Thirty oysters and a congius of garum, sir," Pete responded briskly.

"OK," Snottius replied slowly, disappointed that Pete had got it right. "Anyway, on with the list."

More weird and wonderful ingredients poured from Snottius's mouth. They surprised and disgusted Pete in equal measure.

"Fifty snails, ten eels, two hares, a swan," the chief slave continued.

Pete's head began to swim. Fortunately, Julius was listening intently.

As the boys travelled to town they chattered excitedly about what Iolus might have for Julius.

"Maybe it's loads of money?" Pete suggested with eyes as wide as plates. "Boudicca's money," he added in an excited whisper. "Then you can buy your freedom!"

Julius laughed. "It won't be anything like that, Pete. It might be something of my dad's, like a piece of clothing or something like that."

Although Julius said this in a very offhand way, Pete could tell that he was excited.

"This is perfect," Pete continued. "We're going to get to see Iolus and we haven't had to do anything naughty to manage it."

"Yeah!" Julius replied with a smile. He was much more

relaxed now that he was going to be able to see Iolus. He was desperate to see him again, even though he had dismissed Pete's previous suggestions that they should go back without permission. Now, he was going to see Iolus again *and* he was going to do it without having to sneak out.

They arrived in Camulodunum and Julius tied up the horse and cart near the market.

"We'll get the shopping later," Julius explained to Pete. "Let's see Iolus first."

Julius was taking control now for the first time and Pete smiled to himself at this. It felt like things might be coming together.

They went back to the tavern and Iolus waved excitedly at them when he saw them.

"I'm glad you could make it," he told the boys as they came to his table. "I've got something that is very important to your family." Iolus turned to his side to reach for a pouch tied to his waist. He took something out of it and slowly turned back to the boys.

Pete nudged his friend and whispered, "Here we go. Boudicca's treasure."

Iolus put his hand out and opened his fingers painfully slowly to reveal a circular object. His eyes lit up as he looked at the boys.

"What is it?" Pete asked.

"It is Lugobelenus's official brooch," Iolus explained. "Your father gave it to me the day he disappeared. It shows that he is a member of the Royal Family of the Iceni. Just like you, young Caratacus. This will prove who you are."

Julius sat open-mouthed, staring at this piece of jewellery which had belonged to his father.

Suddenly, a disturbance nearby interrupted them. All three of them looked up to see two Roman soldiers standing next to a man who was pointing at Iolus. The soldiers started walking over to their table. Iolus hurriedly put away Lugobelenus's brooch in the pouch.

"You're coming with us!" one of the soldiers said to Iolus as the other grabbed him by the arm. Pete recognised them as the guards from Noxius Maximus's palace. Fortunately, they didn't seem to recognise him.

They led Iolus into the middle of the tavern and said loudly to everyone who was now watching, "This is what you get for plotting rebellion."

One of the guards, whose name Pete remembered was Scythicus, punched Iolus and he fell on the ground. Then both soldiers picked him up and led him away.

"Let's see what Noxius Maximus has to say about this," Scythicus said loudly for all the tavern to hear.

Pete and Julius looked at each other in dismay.

Chapter 35

T HE TWO BOYS DASHED BACK to the cart. "We'd better get out of here," Julius said. "We don't want any more trouble."

"What about the shopping?" Pete suddenly remembered. "We *will* be in trouble if we don't get that."

Both of them had completely forgotten that they had actually been sent to town to get food for the upcoming banquet.

"Well remembered, Pete!" Julius exclaimed, slapping himself on the forehead. "Right, um, let's go," Julius said, turning back towards the market, but clearly still thinking about Iolus and what he had told them.

"What do we have to get?" Pete asked. "I dunno why they don't just write it down for us. Save us remembering."

Julius looked at Pete quizzically. "Write it down for us?" he asked, stopping in his tracks. His expression told Pete that this seemed a rather bizarre suggestion to him.

"Well, yeah," Pete replied.

"What good would that do us? How would we read it?" Julius asked incredulously.

"What do you mean?" Pete asked, just as confused as his friend. "Can't you read?"

"What? You mean that *you can*?" Julius asked with a dismissive laugh.

"Yeah," Pete replied, hurt by Julius's response.

"Oh, right," Julius said, perplexed by this news. Then his face lit up. "Wow, you can *read*? How did you learn?"

"You know, like everybody else, I guess," Pete replied casually. "Anyway, we better get that shopping."

This was the first time that Pete had been keen to get shopping in his life. He was starting to worry that Snottius might get suspicious if they were away too long. "Let's go. I'm sure we'll remember as we go along."

Pete strode off with Julius following close behind and looking at him with admiration. This was the first time that anyone had looked at Pete with admiration, and it made him feel a little uncomfortable.

Pete was too focussed on getting the shopping done to notice the strangeness of the market this time. Indeed, he didn't even squeal when they went to the butcher.

"I hope we've remembered everything," Pete said to Julius as they returned to the cart and put the shopping into it. Julius had remained silent throughout most of the shopping: he had been shocked by the news that Pete could read and wasn't sure whether to be impressed or disbelieve him.

Julius got up into the driver's position and the cart pulled away.

"Well Pete, you'd better not tell Snottius you can read. He won't like that," Julius warned him with a laugh. "He thinks he's better than all of us." Then Julius paused, deep in thought. He then continued in a slightly sadder voice, "And if Master knows you can read he might sell you on again. That will make you worth a lot more. And then I'll be alone again." Julius said the last sentence very mournfully.

Pete was touched by the fact that Julius seemed to be upset at the thought of losing his friend. Obviously he was forgiven for all the previous trouble. He was then shaken from this pleasant thought by a horrid memory.

"What about Iolus?" he exclaimed with a start and sitting bolt upright in the back of the cart.

"Oh, yeah," Julius replied with concern. He had completely forgotten about the unfortunate man after getting the shock of Pete's admission that he could read.

"Noxius Maximus will torture him!" Pete cried with dread.

"What? Oh no. Really?" Julius asked with terror on his face. "It's my fault, Pete. He wouldn't have been there if he hadn't been meeting us."

"It can't be your fault. He's the one that said we should meet there. It just happened," Pete tried to reassure his friend.

"Poor Iolus." Julius sighed as he geed up the horse to go faster.

The boys continued the journey in silence, lost in thoughts of the man who had tried to help Julius and trying to work out how they might help him.

Chapter 36

"**Y**OU TOOK YOUR TIME," SNOTTIUS sneered at the boys as they got down from the cart. "I was going to send out a search party. Although not even *you boys* would be so stupid as to try to escape again," he cackled. He then looked at Pete and said, "Actually, I'm not so sure that *you* aren't *that* stupid."

The two boys just ignored the chief slave and took the shopping into the kitchen where Caradocus was sitting. He looked very much 'the worse-for-wear' as Pete's mum would have said.

"Hello boys," he croaked as the two of them unloaded the shopping. "Thanks for going to town for me. I couldn't even have got past the entrance to the estate," he said with a weak laugh.

"Are you OK?" Pete asked, not realising that the answer was obviously 'no'.

"Yeah, I'm all right. Snottius gave me merry hell and was all for flogging me. But Probus stopped him," Caradocus explained, rubbing his forehead. He then brightened a little. "Probus said 'You don't treat the finest cook outside of Italy like a common criminal'," Caradocus continued with clear pride in his voice.

"There, you see, Pete. I told you Probus was OK for a slave-master," Julius said.

The boys helped Caradocus prepare dinner, although he wasn't his usual effective self. As the boys cleared the dining table, Probus was told that he had a visitor and left the dining room.

Once they had finished, Caradocus asked Pete and Julius if they would take some drinks and snacks into Probus and the visitor. There were two honey-glazed dormice on the plate which Caradocus handed to Pete. Pete's mouth began to water. He hadn't had any dormice since the unfortunate events in the barn.

As they approached Probus's reception room (the same room where Superbus had embarrassed himself), Pete stopped dead outside. He recognised a high-pitched whining voice coming from within.

"Noxius Maximus," Pete said under his breath.

"What is it, Pete?" Julius asked, but Pete didn't respond, as he was listening to what the high-pitched voice was saying.

"Come on, Probus. You know as well as I do they'll just waste the tax money on some war or some public building," Noxius Maximus could be heard saying.

There was no response from Probus, so Noxius continued: "All you have to do is move the boundary posts of your land before the tax inspector comes. He'll record that you have less land than you actually do have. You'll get charged less tax and I'll cover for you if there's any suspicion. Who won't believe *me*?"

Noxius's voice paused as if awaiting a response from Probus, but there wasn't one.

"Don't you see, you fool? We split the savings. The money isn't wasted on some pointless public project. Everyone's happy!" Noxius concluded with a clap of his hands.

"Come on, Pete," Julius prompted his friend. He clearly hadn't heard what Noxius was saying or didn't understand it.

"Oh, OK," Pete said, remembering the platter of snacks in his hand.

Julius knocked and Probus replied, "Enter!"

"Where have you been?" Probus asked the boys as they entered with the wine and snacks. "Our guest is just *leaving*," he continued, turning and looking at Noxius meaningfully.

"Oh, yes, so I was," Noxius snarled back at Probus, "but not before I've sampled my most *gracious host's* hospitality," he added as he picked up a cup of wine. "Umm, delicious. Reminds me of home. *Is* it Italian?"

"It is," Probus replied curtly, not wishing to engage Noxius in conversation.

"Umm, good. None of that Gaulish or Spanish rubbish," Noxius drawled as he polished off the rest of the wine. "Right, well, I can't spend all evening here. I have *business* to attend to," Noxius said with a malevolent gleam in his eye.

Noxius replaced the cup on the tray that Julius was carrying and Probus called Snottius to show the guest out.

"Well, boys," Probus said with a chuckle as he noticed the two of them still standing there holding out their trays. "I think you can go."

Pete had been rooted to the spot throughout.

A plan was forming in his mind.

Chapter 37

"**W**OW, CAN YOU BELIEVE THAT?" Pete asked Julius once they were alone again.

"What, Pete?" Julius asked, oblivious of what his friend was talking about.

"Noxius Maximus, hey? Trying a tax fiddle," Pete responded. He had heard his dad using the term 'tax fiddle' in the past and it sounded like that was just what Noxius was up to.

"How d'you know that, Pete?" Julius asked, shocked.

"'Cause he said he was doing a fiddle to Probus, duh," Pete replied, incredulous at his friend's stupidity.

"What? You could understand all they were saying?" Julius asked, astonished.

"Well, yeah," Pete replied and then realised that just because he understood everyone, it didn't mean that everyone else understood everyone else.

These underpants are pretty handy, he thought.

"Wow, you understand Latin *and* you can read! You're amazing, Pete. And I thought you were pretty dense when we first met." Julius stopped and shook his head in disbelief.

Pete didn't know whether to be flattered by the compliment

he had just been paid or insulted by the fact that Julius had thought that he was dense previously.

Julius continued, "I only understand a few words of Latin. I think Caradocus knows a bit more. Snottius is the only slave who can speak it properly I think."

Until this point Pete hadn't appreciated that the Britons and the Romans might be speaking different languages!

Pete didn't want to dwell on this, as it might prompt more questions from Julius that Pete would struggle to answer.

"But, yeah, this tax fiddle thing," Pete went on. "I mean, it's pretty exciting. We can use this."

"What do you mean, Pete?" Julius asked, looking at his friend with expectation. He was now rather impressed with Pete and was hanging on his every word.

"Well, we can blackmail Noxius into releasing Iolus. If he doesn't, we'll tell on him about the taxes," Pete explained with satisfaction spreading across his face.

"Oh," Julius grunted in disappointment.

"What?" Pete asked, surprised by the lack of enthusiasm with which his plan had been greeted.

"Who are *we* going to tell on Noxius to, Pete? We're just slaves. Who's going to believe us?" Julius reasoned with his friend.

"Well, OK then," Pete agreed, coming back to earth with a bump.

"Hang on a sec," Julius suddenly started, grabbing Pete's shoulder. "You can read, yeah?"

"Yeah," Pete replied, bored now with Julius's amazement at his gift.

"Well, can you write?" Julius asked with his eyes lighting up.

"Uh, *yeah*!" Pete confirmed, missing the point of Julius's excited questioning.

"Can you write *Latin*?" Julius added just to be sure.

"I guess," Pete replied slowly. He knew he could speak Latin when he was wearing the underpants, but could he write it? How would he know? Everything sounded and looked like English to him.

"Great!" Julius exclaimed, clapping his hands together in glee. Then, lowering his voice in case anyone should hear him, he continued, "I have a plan, Pete."

It was now Pete's turn to look at his friend with excited expectation.

Chapter 38

"**W**ELL, JULIUS?" PETE ASKED, ENCOURAGING his friend to go on.

"Well, the tax inspector is coming tomorrow to see Probus, right?"

"Right," Pete confirmed with a shrug of the shoulders.

"OK. So, he's going to be staying here while he visits other places around this area," Julius explained.

"OK. And?" Pete replied, nodding vigorously, impatient for Julius to come to the point.

"Now, if he finds out what Noxius is up to, then he can do something about it. Caradocus said he's been sent by the new guy who's Noxius's boss. This new boss guy's been sent by the Emperor in Rome and he wants to know how much tax he can collect," Julius explained.

"Yeah, but you said no one would believe us, Julius," Pete reminded his friend.

"Well, yeah, if some slave boy just walks up to the tax inspector and starts accusing Noxius Maximus of a tax fiddle then he'll think it's a joke. He'd probably have you flogged," Julius agreed.

"Yeah, exactly," Pete replied.

"That's where the writing comes in. If we manage to get a note in Latin to the tax inspector, he'll assume someone worth listening to has written it," Julius said with a big smile.

"Maybe," Pete replied noncommittally. "I guess it's worth a go." He was clearly underwhelmed by Julius's plan.

"I'll get some wooden tablets and a pen from Master's study. I know where he keeps it all," Julius said.

"But that's right next to Master Probus's bedroom," Pete gasped.

"I know," Julius replied with a casual shrug and disappeared out of the storeroom in which they were *meant* to be sleeping. It was now late and the rest of the household had gone to bed.

Pete was surprised by Julius's newfound fearlessness. He waited nervously for his friend to return. If he was caught sneaking around by Probus's bedroom, Julius would be in *huge* trouble. Minutes passed and Pete waited and waited. He was very concerned for his first-century friend's safety. The silence was suddenly broken by a yell.

"What's that?" came a voice from the darkness. Then there was silence and then a loud snore. Pete breathed deeply. *It must have been Caradocus calling out in his sleep.*

Pete was now so on edge that he almost screamed when a shape appeared in the doorway of the room. It was Julius.

"Got 'em!" Julius whispered in triumph as he waved the pen and wooden tablets in the darkness. "Now to write that note." He passed the wooden tablets, pen and an inkpot to Pete. "Let's get going."

"But I can't see a thing in this darkness," Pete protested. "How can I write if I can't see?"

"Good point," Julius agreed.

"I'll have to write it once it's daylight," Pete suggested.

"But we can't wait. I have to return the inkpot and pen before Master sees it's gone," Julius protested, suddenly losing his fearlessness.

"I'll do it as soon as it's daylight and then we can get the inkpot back before they realise," Pete reassured his friend.

And so the two of them waited for dawn, unable to fall asleep, afraid that they might miss their chance. They jumped at the slightest sound, knowing that if they were found with the pen, inkpot and wooden tablets it would cause more trouble than they could explain.

Then dawn began to break and Julius started dictating the note to Pete.

"Oooh! The ink's brown!" Pete exclaimed.

"What did you expect? Bright blue?" Julius quipped, unaware that that was exactly what Pete was expecting. "Anyway, we'd better hurry up."

Pete had no idea if what he was writing was English, Latin or Swahili, but he kept going anyway. Julius watched in wonder as his friend wrote. Although Pete had told him he could write, Julius couldn't quite believe it until this moment. Writing on the wooden tablets felt strange and was harder than writing on paper with a good-old ballpoint pen. Julius had to slow down his dictation to allow Pete to catch up. Finally, Pete finished.

"There, all done," Pete said, holding up the wooden tablets to Julius for inspection.

"I can't read it, Pete," Julius reminded his friend with a chuckle.

Suddenly there was a bang further up the corridor and they heard Snottius telling another slave off.

"You clumsy oaf! Are you still not awake?" Snottius could be heard berating his poor victim.

Julius grabbed Pete's arm and they both swallowed hard.

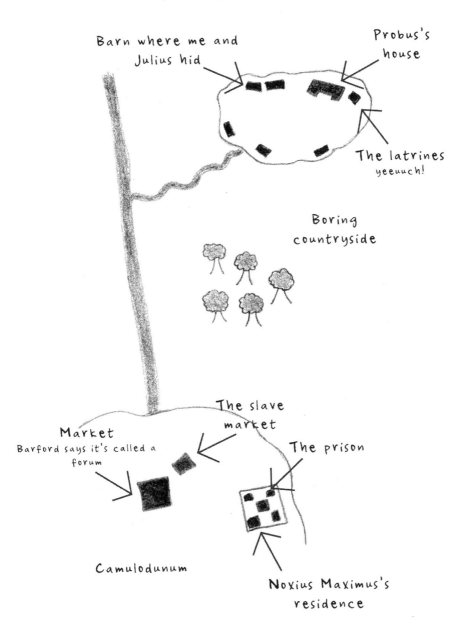

Map of Camulodunum and Probus's estate

Barn where me and Julius hid

Probus's house

The latrines
yeeuuch!

Boring countryside

The slave market

The prison

Market
Barford says it's called a forum

Camulodunum

Noxius Maximus's residence

Chapter 39

PETE GRABBED THE INKPOT, PEN and wooden tablets and shoved them under his straw mattress, just as Snottius walked past the storeroom.

"What are you two lazy morons doing? Get up and get to work. Our guest will be here in a couple of hours!" Snottius barked at the two of them and then stormed off.

Fortunately, Snottius was too preoccupied with the imminent arrival of the tax inspector to notice that Pete's mattress had a suspicious bulge underneath it. Fortunately, he also hadn't noticed (but neither had Pete or Julius) the pool of ink which was expanding from beneath the mattress.

"Pete! The ink!" Julius cried as he noticed the browny-grey lake seeping towards him. The boys quickly picked up the straw mattresses and turned up the overturned inkpot before all the ink had run out. They then desperately started trying to mop up the ink and squeeze it back into the pot, but it was no use: they would never get it all.

"Oh, Pete. What have you done?" Julius groaned.

"Me?" Pete asked incredulously. "This was *your* idea," he reminded Julius.

"To write the note, yeah. But not to wait till daytime and not to knock the inkpot over," Julius whined.

"Stop, stop," Pete pleaded, holding up his hands. "We can argue later. Right now we've got a lot of ink on our hands."

"You're right," Julius agreed, looking around for something. "A-ha!" he said as he spotted what he was looking for. He picked up a bucket from beside a cupboard in the corner of the room and disappeared.

Pete sat horror-stricken beside the now drying pool of ink. If anyone came in, he was for it. Fortunately, with the commotion of preparing for the tax inspector, no one did. Julius reappeared with the bucket full of water and a rag.

"Let's see what we can do with this," he said as he started scrubbing up the ink with the wet rag. In no time most of the ink was gone. There was still some visible, but it blended in with the rough floor of the storeroom. *Thank goodness it wasn't bright blue ink*, Pete thought.

"Right," Julius said, taking a deep breath. "Now to get this pen and inkpot back to Master's study without anyone noticing."

Julius disappeared off again and Pete could almost feel his heart bursting out of his chest. He couldn't take much more excitement.

Then he remembered his mattress, which had been sitting in the pool of ink, but which they had moved to the side of the room in order to clean up. There was a large ink patch on the underside of it. How was he going to explain that?

"What's up, Pete?"

Pete jumped and turned to see Julius behind him. He breathed an enormous sigh of relief.

"Oooh. Yeaahhh," Julius muttered as he spotted the large, brown ink stain on the bottom of Pete's straw mattress. "We're going to have to get rid of it," Julius suggested with a definitive nod of the head.

"Where am I going to sleep, Julius?" Pete protested.

"On the floor," Julius helpfully replied with a shrug. "It will be more comfortable than what will happen to you if anyone finds out about us and the ink."

Pete begrudgingly agreed. Sleeping was going to be even more uncomfortable now in 'the land of the underpants'.

Chapter 40

JULIUS POKED HIS HEAD OUT of the storeroom and looked up and down the corridor. There was no one to be seen so he motioned to Pete to bring the mattress out. Just as Pete emerged into the corridor, Caradocus appeared.

"There you two are!" he cried with a mixture of annoyance and relief. "I thought I was going to have to prepare for the tax inspector's arrival on my own! Oh, hello. What have you got there, Pete?" Caradocus pointed at the bundled up mattress that Pete was holding.

"Um, oh," Pete stumbled on, "my mattress needs airing," he said with a doubtful look on his face. He didn't feel like he was being very convincing.

"I'm not going to ask," Caradocus replied with a chuckle and a shake of the head. "Go and put it outside then and Julius, you come with me," Caradocus instructed as he walked back into the kitchen.

As Pete started to walk off down the corridor, Caradocus called from behind, "Be quick, mind, there's lots to do!"

Pete hurried down the corridor and into the granary. Fortunately, he passed no one else. As he got outside he tore open the mattress and threw the hay out willy-nilly. The wind began to blow it away. Then he threw the ink-stained mattress cover into the corner of the granary.

He hurried back to help Caradocus and was put to work preparing vegetables. He then remembered the note he had written. Where were the wooden tablets? He tapped himself all over to see if he had poked it into his clothes, but to no avail. He would have to wait until Caradocus wasn't looking so he could sneak back to the storeroom to find it. Normally Caradocus was pretty relaxed, but he was really working the boys hard today.

"Snottius has been on at me to make sure this banquet is a success, so please, boys, no messing around, yeah?" Caradocus pleaded with them as he bustled around the kitchen.

Another hour passed and Pete was on tenterhooks. What if someone had found the tablets? He tried to concentrate on the vegetables, but he was starting to panic.

After what seemed another age, Caradocus finally said, "Well, boys, nature calls. Keep up the good work," and he disappeared off to the latrines.

"I just need to go to the storeroom," Pete whispered to Julius. "Back in a minute."

"What? You heard Caradocus. We need to keep working. This is no time for a nap," Julius admonished his friend.

"But I left the tablets in there," Pete explained very slowly and very quietly.

"You what?" Julius exclaimed, his face betraying his panic. "Go! Go!" he said hurriedly, shooing Pete away.

Fortunately, everyone was so busy preparing for the arrival of the tax inspector that they didn't notice our hero sneaking into the storeroom. He looked around and couldn't see the tablets. His heart started thumping in his chest. Just as he was about to turn around and explain to Julius his mistake, he saw the corner of something poking out from under a cupboard. He got down on his knees and pulled it out.

It was the wooden tablets!

Chapter 41

JULIUS ALMOST FELL OVER WITH relief when Pete returned with the tablets. Pete tucked them carefully into his time-travelling underpants beneath his tunic and then focussed on his chores. He couldn't wait to put Julius's plan into action, even if he wasn't sure it would work.

Finally, the tax inspector arrived. Probus and Snottius went out to greet him while the rest of the slaves completed the final preparations. The tax inspector was ushered through to Probus's reception room (where the boys had seen Noxius a matter of days before) and Snottius came to the kitchen to ask for drinks and snacks.

"Use the best **Samian ware**, will you?" Snottius ordered. "This is an important guest and we need to impress."

Caradocus brought down some orange cups and bowls from a locked cupboard. He handed them to the boys and said, "Careful. Master brought these all the way from Italy."

Pete picked up one of the cups and looked at it. It was even fancier than the special plates that Mum only brought out when guests came. There were figures of men all around the side. They were carrying food to another man who was in a toga and lying on a couch. Pete chuckled to himself as he thought it was basically a picture of him, Julius and Probus.

"Now's our chance," Julius whispered to Pete as Pete stared at the cup. Julius then motioned to the wooden tablets tucked underneath Pete's tunic, reminding our hero of their plan.

Pete tapped his underpants to check that the tablets were still there and then the two of them picked up their trays of wine and snacks and stepped forward.

"Where do you think you're going?" Snottius asked the two boys.

"To take the drinks and snacks," Pete replied matter-of-factly.

"The tax inspector's too important to be served by you. Noxius Maximus wasn't impressed by having you two serve him. He told me so himself as he left," Snottius explained smugly as he took one of the trays off Julius. "I'll return for the other tray in a moment," Snottius added with an unpleasant smirk.

"How are we going to get the tablets to the tax inspector now if we aren't allowed near him?" Julius complained to his friend. They both looked at the floor dejectedly.

After an hour or so, Snottius returned to the kitchen and announced, "The tax inspector has started his inspection, so you can clear away now."

Pete then remembered what his Auntie Cheryl had told him: *Opportunities present themselves when you least expect it.*

He turned to Julius and smiled. "Now's our chance," he whispered with conviction.

When they had finished helping Caradocus wash up, Pete said casually, "Nature calls."

Caradocus chuckled and replied, "I think that's allowed now. We've got a good half hour until we need to start preparing for this evening's banquet."

Julius whispered to Pete, "Good luck," and patted him on the back reassuringly.

Pete walked out of the kitchen and made his way towards the latrines at the back of the house. Just before he got there he turned right and made his way towards the fields. He looked around, but there was no sign of the tax inspector, so he walked on.

He walked and walked, but saw nothing. He hadn't realised how big Probus's estate was until now. He was starting to worry: he had been gone quite a while for a toilet trip.

Back in the kitchen, Julius was getting nervous.

"Where's Pete?" Caradocus asked with concern. "We'll have to start dinner soon."

"Oh, uh, I think he's got a tummy bug," Julius explained with a look of feigned sympathy on his face.

"Oh, right. Oh, OK," Caradocus mumbled, rather embarrassed and wishing he hadn't asked in the first place.

Back in the fields, Pete was starting to give up hope and

turned back towards the house. A few hundred metres from the building Pete came to the brow of a hill and his heart leapt. He saw the tax inspector with two men in the distance. He started running over to them, but then realised that this would look suspicious and slowed down to normal walking pace. When he got close he noticed that one of the men was taking long strides along the side of a field away from the tax inspector and the other man. The tax inspector was calling things out to the other man beside him, who was noting them down on wooden tablets just like the ones which Pete had used.

Pete slowed right down and put his hand into the time-travelling underpants (which, fortunately, he was wearing over his own underpants) to feel for the tablets. They were still there. He breathed deeply to calm himself and walked right up to the tax inspector. Just at the moment he passed him he slipped the tablets into the tax inspector's belt and walked on whistling. He thought this would make him look incredibly natural and casual.

Just as he had passed the tax inspector, Pete heard him call out, "Hey, that slave just gave me—" then Pete turned to see why he had suddenly stopped talking.

He saw the tax inspector reading the tablets. The other two men looked at the tax inspector expectantly, but he said nothing else.

He just stared at the tablets.

Chapter 42

P ETE GOT BACK TO THE house after about an hour's absence to find Julius and Caradocus busily preparing dinner.

"Oh, hi Pete," Caradocus said as he walked in. "How's the tummy?"

Pete looked confused at the cook's odd question, but then noticed Julius nodding enthusiastically at him, prompting him to reply.

"Oh, uh, better now," he stammered. "But ooo-eee you wouldn't have liked to be there," he continued, really getting into the cover story now.

"Yeah, OK. Thanks Pete," Caradocus replied, clearly not at all grateful for Pete's additional colouring to the tale. "Anyway, Julius needs your help," he continued, dismissing our hero with a wave of the hand.

"Did you do it, Pete?" Julius asked with bated breath.

Just as Pete was about to respond, Snottius entered the kitchen and clapped his hands to gain everyone's attention.

"Stop, stop, stop!" the chief slave cried, waving his hands at Caradocus and the boys. "The tax inspector has changed his plans and is beginning his visits to other estates *right now*. The banquet is off ... For now. That is all."

Snottius gave each of them a very superior look and then turned and walked off. Snottius was highly annoyed by the tax inspector's decision, as he was very keen to impress him with the banquet. Caradocus had claimed that it was because Snottius wanted to gain attention for himself in the hope that he might be bought by a more important master.

Julius turned and looked at Pete with an excited smile. "He saw the tablets then?" he asked.

"He did," Pete confirmed nonchalantly.

"And that's why he's started his visits now?" Julius prompted his friend.

"I dunno," Pete responded with a shrug of the shoulders.

"I bet that's why," Julius said, more to himself than to Pete.

"Right, boys. You heard Snottius," Caradocus interrupted. "Banquet's off. And after all that hassle from Snottius too!" he moaned. After a pause, his face brightened and he clapped his hands together in satisfaction. "Nap time!" he exclaimed and walked out of the kitchen. As he was about to walk through the door, he turned around and said, "Oh, yeah. Boys, can you tidy up? Cheers." He walked out before they could respond.

"What a cheeky beggar," Pete said to Julius after Caradocus was out of earshot.

"Yeah, he is," Julius agreed with a chuckle.

The boys didn't mind clearing up on their own as it gave them a chance to talk about what had just happened ... And to nibble on some honey-glazed dormice.

"So, now the tax inspector knows all about Noxius Maximus. We're going to get a big reward for this I reckon."

Pete rubbed his hands together as he thought about what that reward might be. An *Xbox Mini* with ten games? That was unlikely: he suspected the Romans didn't have such things. They didn't even have electricity.

How rubbish is that?

"I hope so, Pete. But what if they don't believe us and accuse us of lying?" Julius was suddenly gripped by fear. "What if they think we're just trying to cause trouble and throw us in prison with Iolus?"

Pete hadn't thought of this either and was a little worried now. He certainly didn't want to go back to Noxius Maximus's prison.

"It would be *my* fault this time, Pete," Julius continued, looking forlornly at his friend. The boys continued tidying (and eating) in silence for the next couple of hours, worried about what might happen to them.

They were just finishing and about to go off to bed, when Snottius entered. "Pete! The tax inspector wants to see *you*!" he almost screamed.

Pete looked at Julius and Julius mouthed, "Sorry," at him.

"Come on, you little weasel! How dare you keep such an important official waiting?" Snottius barked.

"How do you know he wants *me*?" Pete whimpered.

"He asked for the odd-looking slave-boy. It can't be anyone else," Snottius explained with contempt. "Come along now!"

Chapter 43

ETE TROTTED ALONG AFTER SNOTTIUS, who stormed ahead of him. The chief slave led Pete to the reception room and knocked. Probus replied very sternly, "Enter!"

Pete took a deep breath and followed Snottius in. Probus and the tax inspector were sitting at the end of the room looking expectantly at the two slaves. The tax inspector was wearing different clothes this time: a very grand-looking toga with two purple stripes around the edge. Pete didn't realise it, but this meant that he was a very important person. The purple dye alone had probably cost a hundred times what Probus had paid the slave-dealer for Pete.

"Apologies for keeping you waiting, my good sirs," Snottius whined smarmily, wringing his hands. "This little piece of trash has no respect," he explained, indicating Pete dismissively with his hand.

"Yes, yes, Snottius. Very good," Probus replied impatiently. "Off you go, then."

Snottius looked confused at being asked to leave and stood there for a moment with a trembling lip. He was about to speak, but then stopped himself and left the room.

Probus then turned to the tax inspector and asked, "Is this the boy?"

The tax inspector replied with a nod, "It is."

"Now then, Pete, is it?" Probus asked with a smile on his face.

Pete hesitated. *Was it a trap?* he wondered.

"Uh, uh, yes, sir," Pete replied with his head bowed, not daring to look at Probus or the tax inspector.

"It's OK, Pete. You don't need to be afraid. We just have a few questions for you," Probus explained, motioning towards himself and the tax inspector.

"That's right … And thank you Probus for summoning the slave," the tax inspector began. "Are you the boy who placed some wooden tablets in my belt?" he asked Pete, saying each word very clearly and pointing at our hero and motioning to his belt as if he thought Pete were an idiot (and he might well have been right, but in this instance it was because the tax inspector didn't know how much Latin Pete understood).

Pete was very unsure what to do. He thought that the two of them might be trying out the old 'good cop' trick that Mum and Dad often used on him. That is to say, being incredibly nice and saying things like, "Now, Pete. Just tell us who broke the window. No one's going to get in trouble. We'd just like to know." Of course, it was always a trap and Pete invariably *did* get into trouble.

He decided he couldn't lie though. It was clearly him who had done it.

"Y-y-yes, sir," he stammered, head still down.

"Thank you. And who wrote the tablets?" the tax inspector continued.

"M-m-me, sir," Pete replied, just as nervously.

"What?" the tax inspector and Probus gasped in unison.

"I'm not sure you heard me correctly," the tax inspector said with a condescending laugh. "Obviously he misunderstood," the tax inspector continued, turning to Probus with a grin. "Well, he is a slave, I suppose. Probably doesn't know much Latin. Anyway, who *wrote* the tablets," the tax inspector asked again, turning back to Pete and making a writing motion with his right hand.

"It was me!" Pete cried, confidence suddenly flowing into him. "I wrote it!"

Probus and the tax inspector started whispering to each other and then Probus called for Snottius. When the chief slave arrived, Probus ordered him, "Go and get me some wooden tablets, a pen and my inkpot."

Snottius disappeared and the two men resumed whispering to each other. Pete couldn't make out what they were saying.

Snottius returned with the tablets, pen and inkpot and handed them to Probus.

"That'll be all, thank you, Snottius," Probus said to the waiting chief slave, not even looking up at him. Pete could tell that Snottius was seething at this treatment, but didn't dare say a word.

The chief slave stormed off, muttering under his breath. Probus looked at the inkpot and said, "Oooh. I'm getting rather low on ink. I must have used a lot more than I thought lately."

Pete smirked to himself at the memory of how Probus's ink supply had actually got so low.

Probus turned to Pete. "Come here, Pete," he instructed the anxious boy in front of him.

So Pete walked very slowly up to the two men. "Take this," Probus said, dipping the pen in the inkpot and handing it to Pete. Pete did as he was instructed.

"Now," Probus continued, "write this: My name is Pete."

Pete approached a low table which was in between the two men and looked down at the wooden tablets. He then began to write, and Probus and the tax inspector looked at each other with open mouths.

"Well I'll be..." the tax inspector said, picking up the tablet and inspecting it. "He wasn't lying. A British slave-boy who can write ... and in Latin to boot!" He shook his head in disbelief and passed the tablet to Probus.

Probus took the tablet and then picked up another tablet which was also on the table. Pete recognised it as his note. Probus looked at both notes side-by-side. "That's astonishing. It's his writing all right."

The tax inspector nudged Probus and said, "You'd better look after that slave-boy. He's the most valuable slave in Britain."

Probus nodded silently and looked at Pete in amazement.

Chapter 44

THE TAX INSPECTOR SMILED AT Pete and then chuckled to himself.

"You're probably wondering why I brought you in here, Pete."

It was the first time that the tax inspector had used his name (rather than just calling him 'slave-boy'). This suggested to Pete that it was all OK now.

Pete nodded frantically and the tax inspector went on. "After I read your note, I considered calling you back to ask what all this nonsense was about, but then I had a thought: what if the note was right?" the tax inspector explained, glancing between Pete and Probus.

"Well, I thought, if it *is* true then the evidence will soon be gone. So I decided there and then to start the rest of my inspections straight away." The tax inspector stopped and looked at them both, waiting for approval for his good idea.

Probus had been listening with rapt attention to the tax inspector: he obviously hadn't heard the whole story either. Noticing the tax inspector looking at him he gave a start and said, "What a marvellous idea." It was clear, though, that he had no idea what the tax inspector was talking about.

"I arrived at the first farm and the landowner seemed most worried by my unexpected arrival," the tax inspector continued. "Not long after I started my inspection I came across some slaves trying to move a boundary post."

"Outrageous!" Probus exclaimed.

"Indeed," the tax inspector agreed, nodding vigorously. "My suspicions were aroused and so I confronted the slaves. They admitted that their master had ordered them to do it." He paused for effect.

"Go on!" Probus urged the other man.

Pete jumped in as well, "Yeah, go on, go on."

Probus was too engaged by the tax inspector's tale to care that the slave had just spoken without being asked to do so.

"Well," the tax inspector said, a broad smile spreading over his face, "I told the landowner what I had seen and he confessed there and then. Noxius Maximus had put him up to it so that they could share the tax he would save."

"Well, well, well," Probus said. "I did have my doubts about Noxius, I must say."

"Now, tell me, Pete," the tax inspector asked, suddenly turning very serious. "How on earth did you know?"

"I heard Noxius telling Master Probus here about it," Pete explained confidently.

Probus's face fell and Pete realised he might have made a mistake.

"Is this true, Probus?" the tax inspector asked with a look of shock.

"It is," Probus replied curtly.

"But my master didn't want anything to do with it. He didn't. He didn't!" Pete explained desperately.

"It's OK, Pete," Probus interrupted, holding his hand up to stop Pete speaking. "Noxius Maximus did indeed ask me to do the same thing. But Pete is right. I did refuse."

"That's as may be, but why didn't you tell me?" the tax inspector asked indignantly.

"I had no evidence. For all I knew, once I'd refused, Noxius might decide not to go ahead with it," Probus explained. "Anyway, Noxius is a cruel and deceitful man. I didn't dare accuse him without evidence."

The tax inspector had been looking at Probus very sternly throughout this explanation. When Probus finished speaking, he stopped staring at him and took a deep breath. "I suppose I would have done the same thing in your shoes, Probus. I have heard some nasty rumours about Noxius Maximus."

"What about Noxius Maximus?" Pete asked.

"He's safely under lock and key in his own prison," the tax inspector said with glee.

Chapter 45

"WELL, I MUST GO AND report to the Governor," the tax inspector announced, taking Pete's tablets from Probus. "He will have heard by now: I sent a messenger to Londinium as soon as we arrested Noxius."

The tax inspector rose and Probus asked, "Will you be returning to finish your tour of inspection?"

"Most certainly, my dear Probus. I still need to find out how bad this tax fraud has been," the tax inspector replied. "We've been suspicious about how much tax this area has been paying for some time. That's why his excellency, the Governor, sent me. I will hopefully be back tomorrow evening to enjoy some more of your wonderful hospitality." The tax inspector slapped Probus on the back good-naturedly.

"And as for this young slave," he continued, turning to Pete, "he really is remarkable."

Pete began to blush. "It wasn't just me, sir. My friend Julius helped too. It was his idea in fact."

"Well I never." The tax inspector chuckled. "Educated *and* modest. Those two virtues rarely go together," he commented, turning to Probus. "I'm sure his excellency, the Governor, will want to reward both you and Julius for this great service to the Empire," the tax inspector suggested, tousling Pete's hair like he was a well-behaved puppy.

"Fantastic!" Pete exclaimed, startling the tax inspector. "Oh sir, there's one more thing."

"Yes, Pete?" the tax inspector replied looking quizzically at our hero.

"There was a friend of ours, a man called Iolus. Noxius Maximus put him in prison for no good reason. Can you help him?" Pete pleaded with wide eyes.

"I'll look into it, Pete. But I can't promise anything. I don't know anything about this man. Noxius may have imprisoned him with good cause for all I know," the tax inspector warned Pete.

"Oh, OK," Pete replied disappointedly.

"Right, Probus can you ask your slaves to prepare my baggage and my carriage, please?" the tax inspector requested and started making his way out of the room. "Good bye, Pete. I'm sure we will speak again soon," he added, just before disappearing out of the room.

Probus followed him out of the room, but turned and smiled at Pete before walking through the door. "You may go back to work now." He turned back to the door, but then turned back again and added, "Oh and thank you, Pete. I didn't even know you spoke Latin that well, let alone could write it."

"Well? What happened?" Julius asked excitedly when Pete finally reappeared in the kitchen.

"Noxius is in prison," Pete said in very measured tones.

"What?" Julius almost shrieked with joy. "And what's going to happen now?"

"The tax inspector is going back to Londinium to tell the Governor, I think he said, about Noxius's tax fiddle," Pete explained. He then told Julius what had happened in his audience with the tax inspector and Julius giggled, gasped and applauded as appropriate throughout.

"I hope they free Iolus," Julius said regretfully once Pete had finished. He then broke into a smile. "I wonder what our reward will be?"

"Dunno. The tax inspector did say he *thought* the Governor would reward us. He didn't say he definitely would," Pete replied, tempering Julius's enthusiasm.

"Oh, I suppose you're right, Pete. I'd better not get my hopes up," Julius agreed.

But the truth is that both boys now had their hopes up sky-high.

Chapter 46

THE BOYS COULD NOT SLEEP that night: Pete because he was now sleeping on the cold, hard floor with no mattress, and Julius because he was just so excited. In spite of saying they wouldn't get their hopes up, they spent the night talking about the wonderful things that might happen.

"I bet they free Iolus and make him like a landowner like Probus," Julius proposed.

"Yeah, yeah. And they make you, like, king 'cause you're Boudicca's nephew," Pete suggested.

"Don't be silly, Pete," Julius replied, but he was secretly pleased with his friend's suggestion.

They passed the rest of the night like this and were still chatting when Snottius appeared in the doorway.

"Here they are then. Master's prize possessions," he spat at the boys. "Lying around like they own the place."

Snottius was trying hard to contain his anger. He blamed the boys for the fact that Probus had treated him high-handedly the evening before. "Get up, you rats!"

He stormed out and the boys smiled at each other. They got dressed and Julius turned to Pete. "There's two things I keep meaning to ask you, Pete."

"Yeah?" Pete answered.

"Where did you learn to read and write Latin?" Julius asked.

"Oh, you know, I just kind of picked it up," Pete replied casually.

"Oh, right. And why do you always wear those weird underpants?" Julius continued.

"Well," Pete answered then paused. He wasn't quite sure what to say. "I guess they're just my lucky pants."

The boys helped Caradocus for most of the day. Probus had rearranged for the banquet to happen that evening, so there was plenty to do. Neither boy could focus and Caradocus had to keep on at them to do their jobs.

"You may be the Governor's star men, but you still have to do your jobs," Caradocus joked.

Caradocus hadn't been at all annoyed when he heard about Pete's gifts and the favour in which he and Julius now found themselves. In fact, he was very pleased for them both. However, he was also a very practical man, and realised that chatting about these things was a waste of time. There was a banquet to prepare.

"Look lively. The tax inspector's back!" Snottius yelled as he walked into the kitchen a few hours later.

"OK, boys," Caradocus said, "we're going to need to be ready in an hour then."

The boys returned to their tasks with more vigour, but before long the tax inspector himself walked into the kitchen.

"Well, well, well," he said and Caradocus and the boys turned around in surprise. It was unusual for even Probus or Superbus to come into the kitchen, let alone an honoured guest like the tax inspector. "We can't have the guests of honour preparing the banquet, can we?"

Caradocus and the boys looked at him in puzzlement. "But you don't need to help, sir," Caradocus explained, highly confused by the tax inspector's words.

"No! I mean Pete and Julius." The tax inspector laughed. The two boys and Caradocus all looked at each other in bewilderment.

"I have news for you which I would like to announce at the banquet," the tax inspector explained.

"You heard the man, boys," Caradocus said. "Guests of honour can't help with the banquet."

The tax inspector smiled at them all and left.

"But what about you, Caradocus? You can't do this on your own?" Julius protested.

"I'll cope. Go along, boys," the cook replied with a good-natured smile.

"No! We'll help you finish!" Pete insisted loudly.

Caradocus looked at the two boys and laughed good-naturedly, his belly shaking. And with that the three of them got back to preparations for the banquet.

Chapter 47

THE TIME CAME FOR THE banquet to begin and Caradocus ushered the boys out of the kitchen. Snottius was waiting outside in the corridor.

"This ways, *sirs*," he instructed the boys with contempt. He had been ordered to accompany the boys to the banquet as honoured guests and was clearly unimpressed.

The only other communication that passed between Snottius and the boys was the occasional snarling glare over the chief slave's shoulder. They stopped outside the now familiar reception room.

"In here!" Snottius barked, indicating the reception room with his head. He then added in a sneer, "*Sirs,*" as he pushed the doors open for them.

"Julius! Pete!" Probus cried joyfully as the two boys entered the room. "Please take a couch," he said, pointing to two empty couches beside the tax inspector, who himself was reclining on another couch. Pete looked around at the strange room. Until this point he had only been into it to take in dishes and clear up after meals.

There was a table full of food in the middle surrounded by leather couches. The walls were painted, just like Probus's reception room, except these paintings were of people eating and drinking: just like the designs on the orange wine cups Pete had seen the previous day. He was surprised by the fact that the tax inspector and Probus were lying down by the table. Mum would not have approved. She always told Pete it was bad for the digestion.

The boys spotted Superbus scowling at the other end of the table. He had been demoted to a less important place, to make space for the boys.

'Well, boys," the tax inspector said, rising with a glass of wine in his hand. "I propose a toast to you both and the service you have done for the Emperor."

Snottius appeared again with a jug of wine. As they now had two slaves fewer this evening, he was being forced to do jobs that would normally be beneath him. He filled the boys' glasses with an expression that looked like he had just smelt the latrine pit (or was remembering the day he fell into it!).

"To the Emperor and to Julius and Pete!" Probus echoed the tax inspector's toast and everyone took a swig of wine. Pete instantly spat his back into the glass. He wondered to himself why adults seemed to like this stuff.

"I propose another toast," the tax inspector continued, ignoring or not noticing Pete's spitting out of his wine. "To Julius's and Pete's freedom."

Though neither Pete nor Julius realised it, just the act of being invited to dinner had shown that they were being granted their freedom.

It was Julius's turn to spit his wine out this time, but not into his wine glass. It went all over the table in front of him, narrowly missing Superbus. The tax inspector and Probus laughed and Superbus muttered under his breath, "That's what you get if you invite barbarians to dinner."

Julius turned red and began apologising profusely. Probus reassured him it was all right. "It happens to the best of us," he said with a wink. He then added, "His excellency the Governor was so impressed with what he heard from the tax inspector about you that he sent money to buy your freedom."

Probus and the tax inspector smiled at the two boys. This was a little bit beyond Julius's level of Latin, so he stood there uncomprehending.

Probus turned to Pete and said, "Maybe you can translate for him."

Pete leaned into Julius and whispered in his ear. A huge smile spread across Julius's face.

"And that's not all," the tax inspector began with a bigger smile than Julius's. "The Governor would like you both to come to Londinium to be educated as Roman gentlemen."

Again Pete translated for Julius and his smile widened even further. It then fell slightly, but Probus and the tax inspector did not notice, as they were toasting each other very liberally.

Pete had noticed, though, and asked Julius what was wrong. "What about Iolus?" Julius asked his friend.

Pete turned to the two men and interrupted their animated conversation. "Excuse me, sirs. What about Iolus?"

"Iolus?" the tax inspector repeated with a blank expression. "Oh, the Briton from the prison. Oh, yes, how could I forget that? That's the most important part," the tax inspector said, rummaging beneath his toga. Eventually he mumbled to himself, "Ah, there it is." And he produced Julius's father's brooch. "I think this belongs to you, young man," the tax inspector stated, handing the brooch to Julius.

"Iolus gave me this brooch when I freed him and asked me to make sure it came to you, Julius. He told me all about your royal ancestry. That is why the Governor wants you to join him in Londinium to be educated as a Roman gentleman," the tax inspector explained with a broad smile.

Julius hadn't understood much of this, but seeing the brooch told him everything he needed to know.

"That scoundrel Noxius had just been locking up Britons willy-nilly," the tax inspector continued. "His excellency, the Governor, would like us to take a much friendlier approach with the locals now," he added, turning to Probus. This friendlier approach included giving a Roman style education to the children of British royalty it seemed.

"Well, boys, we will have to take you tomorrow to be registered as freemen," the tax inspector concluded with a twinkle in his eye.

Chapter 48

P ETE WAS DELIGHTED TO SEE the first course appear: honey-covered dormice. He had devoured three before he even realised it. Probus and the tax inspector watched with ill-concealed amusement. The dormice left Pete feeling rather full (and rather windy, of course). This was fortunate, as the dishes that now followed mostly turned our hero's stomach. He couldn't identify most of them, but the oysters which Snottius had ordered were there and Pete recognised the huge bird served as the main course as the swan that they had bought at the market.

When the meal had finally finished, Julius and Pete were led to a guest bedroom by Snottius. This room actually had raised beds (although they weren't as comfy as Pete's actual bed) and was luxury compared to the storeroom. Julius looked at Pete in wonder.

"Wow, we get to sleep *here?*" Julius gasped in amazement.

Pete feigned amazement too. *It was just a proper bedroom*, he thought. *What was the big deal?*

The two boys lay there talking about the wonderful future that awaited them. Well Julius spoke about it and Pete listened, knowing that he wasn't going to be part of it. He had done his task and so surely would now be going to another period of history and another task.

Once Julius was asleep, Pete sighed regretfully and took off the underpants. He was whisked back into his bedroom in the twenty-first century.

He lay awake, thinking how much he would miss Julius, but also wondering what his next adventure might be. He couldn't sleep, so he decided to find out straight away where he was headed next. He put the underpants back on and was surprised to find himself back in the guest bedroom at Probus's house.

"What? You're kidding me!" he muttered under his breath and took the underpants back off again.

So, it hadn't worked. He hadn't completed his task.

Next day at school he was distracted by thoughts of Julius and Roman Britain. He really thought he had done his task this time. It felt like such an anti-climax. He didn't want to go back now.

That evening he called Auntie Cheryl and told her. He hadn't been in touch with her for a few days, so she was keen to hear everything.

Once Pete had brought her up-to-date, Auntie Cheryl was silent for a moment and then said, "It feels like that should be it." She paused, deep in thought, and then continued. "How did you leave it with Julius?"

"What do you mean?" Pete asked.

"Well, where did you tell him you were going?" she answered.

"Nowhere!" Pete exclaimed in surprise at his aunt. "What was I going to tell him? Bye Julius, I'm just off to the future now," Pete replied sarcastically.

"You have to tell him you're going somewhere else," Auntie Cheryl explained, ignoring or unaware of Pete's sarcasm. "Otherwise you can't leave."

The two of them then discussed what story Pete could tell Julius about why he was going.

That evening at bedtime, Pete put on the time-travelling underpants with determination. He had memorised the story he would tell Julius and was ready to say goodbye. He was back in the bedroom in Probus's house in the blink of an eye.

"Julius, are you awake?" he whispered. He heard some mumbling from the other bed. "Julius, I have something to tell you," he continued.

"Mmm, what?" Julius mumbled back, clearly just waking up.

"I have to go, Julius," Pete whispered, trying to hold back the tears that were starting to form in the corners of his eyes. He had really come to like Julius now.

"You what?" Julius whispered back.

"I'm a spy, Julius, for the Emperor," Pete explained. "I

was sent to catch Noxius Maximus out. They knew he was fiddling taxes, but couldn't prove it."

"What?" Julius asked again and then fell silent. "So that's why you speak Latin and that's why you can read and write," Julius then said, more to himself than to Pete.

"I have to go back to Rome. My job is done," Pete continued.

"What about the tax inspector? Why did we have to go through that elaborate plan to tell him what was going on? You could have just told him," Julius protested, sounding rather aggrieved at the deceit.

"He didn't know. No one knew. It was a top secret mission from Caesar."

Pete felt bad about lying to Julius, but Julius would not have believed the real reason he was there.

"I have to leave before dawn without anyone knowing. You can't tell anyone, Julius. OK?" Pete continued.

"But what about Londinium?" Julius asked. Although Pete couldn't see him in the darkness, he could hear that he was starting to cry. This made it even harder for Pete to control himself. "We were going to go together," Julius moaned.

"But you will still go ... And you will have a great life," Pete suggested and then added with a smile, "they'll probably teach you to read and write."

Julius laughed and choked back the tears. "Yeah," he said with a chuckle. "I'll miss you, Pete."

"I'll miss you too, Julius," Pete responded, giving into his tears now.

Pete removed the underpants and found himself back in

his own bedroom. He stood there with tears running down his face.

He then had a thought. "Has it worked?" he wondered to himself. He reached for the underpants and put them back on. Again he felt his hips being pulled and in a flash of light he suddenly found himself in an open space inside what looked like a castle. There were lots of other people milling around Pete.

Suddenly there was a loud noise like a trumpet and Pete turned around with everyone else to see a man in armour approaching on a horse in a red-and-black chequered coat. He looked like a knight from Pete's *Dragon Dancer* game.

"Make way for Sir Hugo de Ponsonby," a man walking in front of the horse shouted.

"It worked," Pete whispered to himself, half in wonder and half in regret.

Back in the first-century AD, Julius whispered, "Pete, are you still awake?"

There was no answer.

Acknowledgments

I am grateful to John, Sue, James, Emily and Jack for their help and support.

About the Author

Barford lives in London with his wife and his very fat cat. He is also a gigantic history geek, as you may have guessed.

Website
barfordfitzgerald.com

Email
barford@barfordfitzgerald.com

Coming Soon
From Barford Fitzgerald

Coming Autumn 2016: Pete Tollywash (and
his time-travelling underpants) will return
in an adventure in Tudor England

Also by
Barford Fitzgerald

Holly Watson and the furry thieves, Book 1
of the Kelsey Park Detective Agency

Made in the USA
Charleston, SC
05 July 2016